Note to Readers

The Fisk and Stevenson families are fictional, but the mill explosion in Minneapolis actually happened on May 2, 1878. Eighteen men were killed in the disaster that destroyed six flour mills. That same year, Milton L. Rentfrow wrote a song about the accident. "The Minneapolis Mill Disaster" included this verse: *All that was left next morn to tell, Of how those mighty Mills had fell, Was a smoking mass of crumbled walls, Which lay beneath our feet.*

Before rebuilding could begin, a trial was held to decide which came first—the fire or the explosion. If an explosion caused the disaster, the insurance companies wouldn't have to pay for the mills to be rebuilt. The courtroom experiment you read about in this book actually took place during the trial. Because of the mill disaster, new safety measures were put into effect to prevent similar accidents from happening.

THE GREAT MILL EXPLOSION

JoAnn A. Grote

ISBN 1-57748-288-3

Published by Barbour Publishing, Inc.
P.O. Box 719
Uhrichsville, Ohio 44683
http://www.barbourbooks.com

Printed in the United States of America.

Cover illustration by Peter Pagano.
Inside illustrations by Adam Wallenta.

CHAPTER 1

Explosion!

Minneapolis, Minnesota, May 28, 1878

"I dare you, Walter! I dare you to slide down the sluice!"

Walter Fisk glanced from Sherman O'Reily's teasing green eyes to the fast flowing water below them. He shifted his feet, slid his fingers around his suspenders, and tried to act like he wasn't interested. "Aw, it doesn't look so great."

Sherman's laugh sang out over the sound of gurgling water from the sluice and the roar of St. Anthony Falls. "You're just afraid you'll end up going over the falls instead of down the sluice."

Jack's laugh joined Sherman's.

Walter felt his face grow hot. Sherman's words were too close to the truth. The falls were huge. They went almost all the way across the Mississippi River. If a piece of a sluice broke, a boy could wind up in a dangerous place in the mighty Mississippi.

He glanced at the sluice again. Logs were floated down the river from the great forests in northern Minnesota and Wisconsin. The sluices were built for the logs to float around the falls, so they didn't clog the river.

The sluices were each only a few feet wide. Log pillars held the sluices above the river, like a dock. The sluices curved along the Mississippi shoreline.

"My *For* doesn't like boys to ride the sluices," Anton Olson said, running a hand through his wavy blond hair. "Maybe we shouldn't. *For* says it's dangerous."

Walter thought Anton looked nervous about riding the sluices, just like he did. Anton's father owned one of the many sawmills along the river. At Anton's home, Walter had heard Mr. Olson rage in his strong Swedish accent over the boys who rode the lumber sluices.

Sherman snorted. "Why don't you say Father or Papa instead of *For*? You're in America now. You should speak English."

Anton's fair skin turned dark red. "In Sweden, I always called him *For*."

Anger flashed through Walter at Sherman's unkindness. "I guess a boy can call his father whatever he wants."

Sherman just shrugged and brushed at the red, wavy hair above his freckled face. "I've ridden the sluices a lot of times. It's great fun. No one ever got hurt. Anyway, we're all twelve years old and know how to swim. Who cares what your father thinks, Anton? He won't catch us at it."

"Yeah," Jack agreed.

Walter ignored Jack. Jack had dirty brownish-blond hair that always hung in his eyes and over his shirt collar. Jack followed Sherman around all the time. Walter wondered if he ever thought for himself, or if he let Sherman do all his thinking for him.

Sherman was the most popular boy in school and a great baseball player. Walter had been excited when he and Jack joined the Blues, the baseball team Walter started a month earlier. Since then, Sherman had been very friendly, and that meant Walter had a lot of new friends.

"Scaredy cat!" Sherman teased.

Walter tried to hide a shudder. The wooden walls didn't look strong enough to him to separate the sluice water from the river.

Still, he didn't want Sherman to think he was frightened.

He took a deep breath. "I'll do it."

Sherman slapped him on the back. "I knew you would! Let's slip behind the mills and get ready."

Anton's blue eyes looked worried. Walter forced a grin. "Come on, Anton, we can do it."

Anton didn't say anything. He just followed along with the others behind Sherman.

A few minutes later, with their outer clothes piled in a shadowy corner behind one of the mills, the boys raced back to the sluices. The wind bit through Walter's drawers, and he shivered.

Without a glance at the other boys, Sherman climbed into the sluice nearest shore. He grabbed the sides and shoved to get himself started. "Yahoo!"

On his back, he slipped along the wooden chute. Excitement began to build in Walter's chest.

Jack jumped in next, and a moment later was yards down the slippery sluice.

Walter grinned at Anton. "It looks like fun."

Excitement sparked in Anton's eyes, and he nodded. Walter wondered if he'd already forgotten his father's warnings.

Walter took a deep breath. “I guess I’m next.”

He sat down on the side and swung his legs over, thinking the chute looked like a long canoe inside. Rushing water tugged at his feet. Slowly he let himself down into it.

“Whoa! It’s cold!”

Anton laughed nervously.

Walter’s hands clutched the edge of the sluice. He was shivering in his long drawers. “Think we’ll get any slivers in our bottoms from sliding down this thing?”

Anton laughed again, and Walter didn’t think he sounded so nervous this time.

Walter’s heart hammered against his chest, and he wasn’t sure whether it was from excitement or fear or both. “Here goes nothing,” he called, forcing himself to let go of the side.

The water pulled him along, feet first. He had to lie back to keep from knocking his head against the wooden rungs that crossed the top of the sluice every few feet. He went around a bend, sliding up farther on one side of the chute and increasing his speed.

He forgot how cold the water was. He forgot his fear of the river below the sluice. All he could think about, all he felt, was the excitement surging through him at the speed he was moving. It felt faster than riding on his father’s train with the engine going all out.

The chute started down the incline where the land dropped, forming the waterfalls. The roar of St. Anthony Falls pounded in Walter’s ears. Fear rushed back. His heart dropped to his stomach as he plunged down, down, down!

It seemed but a moment later he dropped off the end of the chute into the calm waters at the edge of the river some distance below the bottom of the great falls. He hit the river with a resounding “splash” that left his bottom feeling like he’d just had a whipping.

He swam toward the tree-lined shore, where Sherman and Jack were waiting on a large rock.

"A. . .a. . .augh!"

He turned around in time to see Anton hit the river, water spraying up many feet in the air. He laughed as Anton sputtered to the surface.

"Let's go again," he said as he and Anton climbed up on the gray rock beside his friends. He shivered as the early evening air hit him.

"Too late," Sherman said. "It's after six. The men will be leaving the mills soon, and it will be getting darker. But we can do it another time."

They crawled onto the steep, tree-lined shore that smelled like mud and grass and river. Then they followed a narrow dirt path along the river back toward the falls and the mill where they'd left their clothes.

"That was fun, wasn't it?" Anton asked.

"Most fun I've ever had," Walter agreed, grabbing a gnarled, bent tree root and pulling himself up an incline.

That was just as brave as the things Tom Sawyer and Huck Finn do on the Mississippi River, Walter thought, remembering his favorite book. *I'll never be afraid of anything again. Not anything.*

The boys reached the mill and quickly pulled their outside clothes on over their wet drawers. Then Sherman and Jack headed home.

"Let's not go home yet," Walter said to Anton. "I'd like my clothes to be a bit drier when I get home, so my parents won't guess what we've been doing."

Anton nodded in quick agreement.

The two wandered along the busy riverside. They stuffed their socks into their shoes and went barefooted.

There weren't trees and vines along this part of the river.

Instead signs of man's power over nature were shown in the many businesses using the waterfalls. They wandered past a number of flour mills, a paper mill, a woolen mill, a sash mill, and sawmills.

The great St. Anthony Falls ran the largest businesses in the city, maybe in the state. *Minneapolis might not even exist if it weren't for the falls,* Walter realized.

" 'Go with me, down to the falls,' " Walter started quoting from a popular poem. Anton joined him in finishing it.

And see the power there moving,
Mill stones and saws and countless shafts,
As if 'twere nothing doing.

They grinned at each other as they finished it together. Walter thought Anton's heavy Swedish accent sounded funny mixed with his own plain way of speaking, but he didn't say so. Anton was a good friend. He was glad Anton's family had moved in next door a few months ago, when Anton's father bought one of the sawmills near the falls.

"Let's walk over the bridge," Anton suggested.

Walter readily agreed. He never tired of crossing the busy bridge and looking down on the famous river.

Many of the mills were closed or closing after the day's work. The streets about them were filled with workers in dirty overalls or jeans. Each of them carried the tin bucket in which they'd brought their lunch to work.

Walter knew a number of the men, many of whom lived in his neighborhood. They greeted him with smiles and friendly slaps on the shoulder.

Minneapolis felt like home now, he realized. Two years ago he and his family had moved here from Cincinnati. It had taken a long time to get to know people and feel like he lived here instead of just visiting.

They walked between the high limestone towers where the bridge met land. Walter always liked walking between those towers. They were higher than the many-storied buildings beside the bridge. When they passed the towers, wind whipped at their hair and wide shirt sleeves.

Walter shifted his shoulders. "I wish my drawers were dry," he whispered.

Anton laughed. "Mine, too. It's uncomfortable, isn't it?"

"Very uncomfortable!"

Walter tugged at one of his trouser legs. His damp drawers were sticking to his skin. His trousers and white shirt were sticking to his drawers and making them damp, as well. At this rate, the sun would be down before his clothes dried and he could go home without suspicion.

"Walter! Yoo-hoo, Walter!"

At the sound of his cousin Polly Stevenson's voice, Walter turned around. She was with her best friend and next-door neighbor, Brita Swenson.

Polly's curly brown hair had been tied back at one point in the day, but the wind had caught at the curls and pulled them loose. Now her hair hung about her shoulders. Brita's shiny blond braid was wrapped around her head where the wind couldn't play with it.

The wind did catch at the girls' dresses. The wide, ruffled skirts ended below their knees. Polly held a bunch of material in one hand, trying to keep the skirt from blowing.

Walter saw her glance at a fashionably dressed young woman who was passing by. "I can't wait until I'm old enough to wear long dresses like ladies. Their skirts are too long for the wind to blow them above their knees."

Brita giggled. "They look heavy and hot to me."

Walter thought so, too.

Polly sighed. “I think they look elegant and sophisticated.”

Walter laughed. He didn’t think Polly was at all elegant or sophisticated.

“What are you laughing at, Walter Fisk? I’m eleven now, you know, old enough to start thinking about long skirts. Just because boys can start wearing long pants when they’re about ten, doesn’t mean you need to act so superior.”

“What are you two doing here?” Walter asked, thinking it safer to change the subject.

Polly brushed at the curls the wind was tossing into her face. “We walked with Brita’s father to the flour mill.”

“Father is an expert miller,” Brita explained to Anton. “He works at Cadwallader C. Washburn’s flour mill.” She giggled. “I love to say that name.”

Walter looked downriver at the mill district where tall flour mills and grain elevators towered. St. Anthony Falls powered the mills. They were the reason Minneapolis was sometimes called the Mill City.

His father said the mills wouldn’t be so important if it weren’t for the railroads. The farms in western Minnesota sent their grain to the mills on railroads like the one his father worked for. Then the mills ground the grain into flour and sent it all over the country.

The flour mills were the most important industry in Minneapolis. Walter knew Brita had good reason to be proud of her father, who had one of the most important jobs in one of the largest mills in the world.

Polly patted her skirt down as a gust of wind hit them. “Since we were already out, we decided to go for a promenade.”

Walter snorted. “That’s only a fancy word for a walk.”

Polly gave him a withering glance. “All the fashionable women promenade.”

He exchanged an amused glance with Anton. “Shall we

promenade with the ladies, Anton?" he asked in as proper a voice as he could muster.

Anton grinned. "Surely," he said in a voice just as proper.

Brita giggled. Polly grabbed her arm and led her past the boys and along the walkway on the side of the bridge, out of the way of horses, carriages, and wagons clattering across.

Walter rather liked Brita, for a girl. She was almost always smiling, and she was easy to get along with.

After a few minutes, Polly turned around. "Have you seen Uncle Daniel yet, Walter?"

"Not yet."

Walter stopped to look over the edge of the bridge and into the rushing water beneath. The others joined him.

"I didn't know you had an uncle in Minneapolis besides Walter's father," Brita said.

"Yes, Daniel Allerton. He's a doctor," Polly told her, her green eyes dancing with excitement. "He and his wife, Marcia, just moved here from Boston. That's where he went to college, at Harvard."

"Dr. Dan used to live in Cincinnati, like me," Walter said.

"Why did he go all the way to Boston to go to the university?" Brita asked.

Walter shrugged. "Harvard is a good medical school. One of our ancestors, Steven Allerton, was one of the first students there, right after the American Revolution."

Anton's eyes were large. "That long ago? My family only came to America when I was little."

They all laughed. Anton and his family still spoke English with a Swedish accent that told everyone they hadn't lived in America for a long time.

Lots of Scandinavian people came to Minneapolis when they came to America. Some stayed in Minneapolis to find work where they would be close to other people from their homeland.

Other Scandinavians went on to the lands that were opening up for farming in Minnesota and the Dakotas, now that most Indians lived on reservations. Some went west by trains like the ones Walter's father drove. Others went west by wagon train. Walter and Polly had already seen wagon trains of immigrants leaving Minneapolis for the plains this spring. He liked watching the slow-moving, large oxen pulling the wagons that were filled with all the settlers' possessions.

"My parents came from Sweden before I was born," Brita said. She turned to Walter. "You must be glad to have your uncle Dan in town, since you knew him in Cincinnati."

"He's not really our uncle," Walter explained. "He's my father's cousin."

Polly waved a hand. "It's easier to call him an uncle than explain all that." She turned back to Brita. "Anyway, Dr. Dan and his wife have this darling baby, only a year old, named Richard. Aunt Marcia says I might be able to help her with him sometimes."

"We could take him on walks in his perambulator," Brita said eagerly.

Walter looked at Anton and rolled his eyes. "Beats me what girls find so exciting about babies. They can't play baseball or any other fun games."

"They don't do anything but lay around and eat and make messes," Anton agreed.

The boys doubled up in laughter. Polly glared at them. "Boys!" The disgust in her voice made Walter laugh all the harder. "They may be a year older than me and two years older than you, Brita, but we're more grown up than they are."

Still grinning, Walter tugged at his damp shirt.

Polly scowled. "Why is your shirt wet, Walter?"

Walter's heart skipped a beat. *Wouldn't you know she would notice that?* he thought. He tried to think of an excuse that wouldn't be a lie, but he couldn't.

"We, uh, we rode the—"

Boom!

A deafening sound cut off the rest of his sentence. The bridge rocked like a cradle. Walter fell against Anton and then was tossed toward the guardrail. He grabbed it and held on tight as his feet slipped out from beneath him. Fear flooded his chest. "What's happening?" he yelled, but he couldn't even hear his own voice.

CHAPTER 2
The Huge Fire

Walter saw his friends clutching the rail as tightly as he was clutching it. Their feet slid along the rocking bridge as if it were paved with ice.

Was his face as white as theirs? Were his eyes as wide with fear? Their screams mingled with the screams of the people around them.

Is the bridge going to fall? he wondered, fear streaking through him. *Are we all going to be thrown into the Mississippi River?*

If they fell into the river here, they'd be swept over the falls. They'd never live through that!

"Earthquake!" he heard someone yell.

"Earthquake! Earthquake!" people repeated at the top of their voices.

Horses reared and plunged, trying to get off the bridge and away from the buggies and wagons they pulled. The drivers tried to steady them and keep their vehicles from turning over.

One horse dashed up on the walkway, pulling a careening carriage and screaming man along behind him. Walter's heart jumped to his throat. He hugged the railing tighter and tried to stay out of the way of the huge animal. A minute later the animal and carriage moved on down the walkway, rocking all the way.

Clunk!

Thud!

"What is that?" he called to no one in particular. "Ouch!" Something struck him on the top of his head. He let go of the railing with one hand and put up his arm to shield his face and head.

Nothing else hit him, but for a minute, it sounded like large pieces of hail were hitting the bridge. Looking cautiously about, he saw it wasn't hail at all. It was chunks of wood and concrete!

"What's happening?" Polly asked, grasping his arm.

"I think it's an earthquake," he answered when he could get his breath.

The bridge stopped heaving. With a sigh of relief, Walter planted his feet firmly on the walkway again, but he kept a tight hold on the railing with one hand.

People righted carriages. A delivery man collected the tall barrels that had fallen from his wagon and rolled across the street in the middle of the bridge. A man in a fashionable suit checked the leg of the horse that pulled his buggy. Walter wondered whether something falling from the sky had hit the horse, as it had him.

"Everyone is coming out to see what's happened," Anton said.

Walter could see he was right. People poured from the tall buildings lining the roads beside the river. Soon the streets were filled with rushing, confused people.

Women and children in the street and walkway about them were crying. Walter was glad Polly and Brita were too brave to cry.

"Look!" Brita's voice was high and edged with fear.

Walter, Polly, and Anton looked where she pointed. Walter's stomach clenched like someone had grabbed it tight in his fist.

Black smoke billowed from the midst of a cluster of tall mills on the land beside the falls. "The mills!" His voice came out in a whisper.

While they watched, flames shot through the middle of the black smoke, reaching higher against the sky than the tallest buildings. Walter thought that he could hear the roar of the fire above the sound of the river rushing below them and the fierce wind that still tore at their hair and clothes.

The crowd on the bridge went from noisy confusion to silence as they watched the flames.

Then Walter heard his words repeated over and over by the crowd. "The mills! It's the mills!"

Brita's blue eyes were huge. "Papa! What if it's the mill where Papa's working?"

Fear curled in Walter's stomach.

Polly put her arms around her friend's shoulders. "Your father will be all right. It can't be his mill. It can't be!"

But it might be, Walter thought. He watched the red, yellow, and orange flames doing their weird, sickening dance above the buildings between them and the bridge. The curling in his stomach grew tighter.

"Where's the Washburn A building?" Anton whispered in his ear.

Walter couldn't see it. It was one of the tallest buildings in the city, seven-and-a-half stories. It should be easy to see above the shorter buildings around it.

He licked his lips. "Maybe it's behind the fire. Maybe the smoke and flames are hiding it."

But he didn't believe that. He glanced at Brita's face and then away. He didn't want to admit to himself what he believed about that fire.

The crowd began surging toward the massive fire. Walter and his friends started that way, too. They crossed from the bridge into Bridge Square. Two-, three-, and four-story business buildings as well as city hall lined the large square.

Crunch! Crunch!

Walter stopped and stared at his feet. Anton bumped into him. Then Polly bumped into him. Strangers—women in long walking dresses, men in work clothes, and men in suits—jostled them.

"What's the matter?" Anton asked.

"The street is covered with broken glass!" Walter looked up at the tall business buildings. His jaw dropped. "All the glass has fallen out of the windows!"

The others stared. People around them twisted their necks to see, too, but no one stopped. They were all too eager to get to the fire.

So was Brita. She pushed past Walter. "I have to find Papa!"

Walter, Polly, and Anton followed.

The streets were so crowded with people that the horse-drawn carriages and wagons could barely move. Brita dodged around the head of a bay-colored horse, then between a newsboy with his leather bag flapping against his knees and a man from the local meat market in his long, dirty white apron. Then she disappeared from sight.

Walter dashed toward where he'd last seen her bouncing blond braids.

"Wait for me, Walter!" he heard Polly call.

"Hurry!" he called over his shoulder. A minute later he caught up to Brita. "Let's all hold hands," he said, "so we don't lose each other in the crowd."

"All right," Brita agreed, breathlessly, "but let's hurry!"

Polly and Anton caught up to them in a minute, and they all started out again, holding hands. They tried to hurry, but the crowd grew thicker as they neared the mills. The smoke grew thicker, too. It surrounded them like a dirty cloud. It made Walter's eyes water, and he could see it made his friends' eyes water, too. The smell of smoke and sickening odor of burning wheat made Walter's nose burn. Some ladies and men about them were holding handkerchiefs to their noses.

Clang! Clang!

Walter stretched his neck and tried to look over and around the crowd. Where was the loud sound of the bell coming from? "The fire truck is coming!" he called to his friends.

At least it was trying to come. The horse-drawn truck was stuck in the crowd. Firemen and policemen tried to clear a path through the people, but everyone was so intent on reaching the fire that the horses could only move forward a couple feet at a time.

"Why don't they let the firemen through?" Brita cried. "Let them through! Let them through!"

Walter's chest ached for her. "Let the firemen through!" he cried, adding his call to hers. Anton and Polly joined in, and soon the crowd about them picked up the chant. "Let the firemen through!"

The crowd began to make a path, and the horses pulled the truck with its large steam boiler toward the fire that was still blazing away.

Now they were close enough so that cinders fell on them. Walter batted at some that landed on his shirt, burning a black-edged hole through the brown cotton material. Then he grabbed hold of Anton's hand again.

They pushed and dodged their way through the crowd until they couldn't get any closer. The heat of the fire kept people from getting too close. The flames roared so loudly that Walter and his friends had trouble hearing each other speak.

Still, they were close enough to see what was happening. The sight in front of them made Walter sick to his stomach. Many buildings were on fire. The wind was whipping the flames about wildly, spreading burning embers to all the buildings around. But the worst thing he saw was the huge, burning hole in the ground where the Washburn A flour mill once stood.

"It's gone!" Brita whispered hoarsely. Tears filled her eyes. "It's gone! Where's my papa?"

Chapter 3
A Missing Father

I'm going to throw up, Walter thought. How could a seven-and-a-half-story building disappear? Had it fallen down in the earthquake? Or had there been an explosion? Was it an explosion instead of an earthquake that had made the bridge rock?

"Where's my papa?" Brita repeated, tears in her voice.

No one could have lived through the destruction of the mill, Walter thought, but he didn't want to tell Brita.

Firemen were pouring water on the burning hole and the burning buildings around it. The steam and smoke and flames made it impossible to know for sure what they were seeing. The heat from the fires made it almost too hot to stand so close, and Walter realized that his clothes were finally dry.

A man in overalls and a dark, coarse work shirt shoved his

way beside the kids. "I work in that mill on the day shift," he told the man beside him. "Did anyone get out, or were they all k–killed?"

Walter held his breath, waiting for the answer. He saw Brita turn a tear-streaked face filled with hope and fear toward the man.

The man shook his bearded head. "It appears Washburn A exploded. There was no building left for anyone to crawl out of. Some of the men in the nearby burning mills got out, but most of them I've seen were burned or injured."

"No!" Brita covered her mouth with her hand, stifling a sob.

Polly put her arms around her. "Come on, Brita. Let's go home."

"I have to find my papa!"

The bearded man shook his head again. His eyes were filled with sympathy. "If your papa was in one of these mills, you won't be able to find him in this crowd, with the fire and all. Go home, girlie, and wait."

"He's right," Walter said. "I know you want to stay here and find him. I'd want to if it were my father. But we'll never find him in this mess."

"No!" Brita's round chin was set firmly. "I'm going to stay."

"Brita! What are you doing here?"

A wave of relief flowed over Walter. It was Per, Brita's sixteen-year-old brother. He'd know what to do.

Brita grabbed Per's arm. "Have you seen Papa?"

Per put his large hands on Brita's shoulders. "Not yet, but I'll find him. You shouldn't be here." He glanced at Walter, Polly, and Anton. "None of you should be here. It's not safe with this fire and wind."

"But, Papa—"

Per smiled a smile that Walter thought wasn't real. Per's eyes still looked worried. "Go home with your friends, Brita. I'll find Papa or find out if he's been taken to a doctor. I'll come tell you and Mama as soon as I can."

"Promise?"

"I promise. Now go. It will be getting dark soon. Besides, I'll be able to find him sooner if I don't have to worry about you."

"All right." Brita wiped the tears from her soot-smudged face with the arm of her blouse. "But hurry, Per."

Walter glanced at Polly over Brita's head as they wound their way through the crowd toward home. Polly looked as afraid for Brita as he felt. What news would Per have for Brita when he arrived at home? Would he find their father alive or dead?

Polly opened her eyes to the sunshine streaming in through the lace curtains covering her bedroom window. *I feel as tired as when I went to bed,* she thought.

For hours after she'd gone to bed, she'd tossed and turned and been unable to sleep. What had Per found out about his and Brita's father? Would she ever see quiet, nice Mr. Swenson alive again?

She dragged herself out of bed and opened the cupboard where her dresses hung. She chose a dark blue dress with only a few ruffles across the front of the skirt and a small bow at the back of the waist above the bustle. She didn't feel like wearing something bright and cheerful today, not with Brita and her father on her mind.

Polly pulled long cotton stockings over her knees, glad it was spring and she didn't need to wear the itchy wool stockings any longer. After she'd dressed, she brushed her hair, pulling the sides of her hair back with tortoiseshell combs, letting her brown curls tumble down her back.

"Have you heard anything about Mr. Swenson?" she asked her parents as soon as she entered the kitchen.

"Not yet," her father said, "but I'm sure we'll hear something soon."

He winced slightly when he sat down at the oak kitchen table. Polly wondered whether his leg was bothering him. He'd lost a leg in the War Between the States. Sometimes he was a bit stiff in the joints because he didn't have two legs.

Even though it was May, it was often cool on Minnesota mornings. Polly was glad for the warmth of the black iron stove as she slid into her place at the table.

"Let's pray for Brita's family as we say grace," Mama said, sitting down beside Polly.

Oatmeal had been steaming all night on the back of the kitchen stove. It smelled especially good with the cinnamon Polly's mother stirred into it. The cream she poured over it was cold and fresh, delivered to their front step by the milkman that morning.

But Polly was quiet while she ate breakfast with her parents and nine-year-old brother, Abe. Abe, who looked like their father with his curly brown hair and brown eyes, chattered on about the fire, a fishing trip he wanted their father to take him on, where to find the best nightcrawlers, how strict his teacher was, and how much he'd like to play on Walter's new baseball club.

Polly wished he'd shush. *I wish he was more like the quiet man he was named for, Abraham Lincoln,* she thought.

"Better not stop for Brita on your way to school today," Mama advised Polly when she was ready to leave. "I'm sure she'll not be attending. Even if her father wasn't harmed by the fire, the family was probably up late, worrying and waiting."

"But I want to find out about Mr. Swenson."

"I'm sure we'll know what happened by the time you get home from school. You can visit the Swensons with me then."

Polly stared at the two-story, white wooden house next door, where the Swensons lived. Would Brita think it strange she didn't stop to pick her up for school?

It was lonely walking to school without Brita, even though Abe walked with her. Abe chattered all the way. She ignored him.

Concentrating on schoolwork was hard. During a class spelling bee, she was the first student forced to sit down because she misspelled a word. The teacher, Miss Frye, frowned at her. Polly was embarrassed. Usually she was one of the class's best spellers.

At lunch, all the kids were talking about the fire and explosion. Sixteen men had been killed and many injured. Some of the boys had heard horrible stories about men who were killed. The stories made Polly's skin crawl. *They're just making the stories worse than they really are,* she told herself, *because they like to scare the girls in our class.* But she couldn't get the awful stories out of her mind during the afternoon classes.

She'd never been so glad to hear the school bell ring at the end of the day! She hurried home, not even waiting for Abe. The air was foggy with smoke. It made her nose hurt to breathe.

At home, good smells pushed away the fire odor and blended with the nice wood smoke smell of the kitchen stove.

Polly dropped her books on the kitchen table. "Hello, Mother. What are you cooking?" She lifted the lid of a large, cast-iron pot on the stove and sniffed in the mouth-watering scents.

"Chicken stew and dried apple pie. I thought we'd take them to the Swensons' when we go." Mama sighed. "The pie would be better with fresh apples, but we can't expect to find any of them at this time of year. We've eaten all of the apples we stored in the sand barrels in the cellar."

"Your dried apple pies are always good."

"How was school?" Mama asked, tucking a stray red hair behind her ear. As always, her face was flushed from cooking over the hot stove.

"All right. Did you hear about Mr. Swenson yet?" Polly held her breath waiting for the answer. *If the news is bad, I don't want to hear it,* she thought.

Her mother's green eyes shone. "Yes. He's alive."

Polly closed her eyes and took a deep breath. She'd been so afraid for Brita!

"But he was hurt."

A small bit of fear wiggled through Polly's chest. "Very badly?"

Her mother nodded, wiping her hands on the huge white apron that covered her housedress. "I'm afraid so. Daniel attended him. Why don't you ask him about Mr. Swenson? He's in the family living room with Marcia and Richard."

Polly dashed through the swinging door into the dining room, then tore down the hallway, past the door to the parlor, which was used to entertain company, and into the family living room.

Dr. Dan was seated in her father's favorite overstuffed chair, his head resting against the high back, his eyes closed. Marcia, seated in the small rocker with its back and seat upholstered in pretty fabric with roses, was rocking Richard. Richard had black hair like his father. It stood out against his mother's rose-colored dress.

Marcia smiled at Polly and whispered, "Both my men are sleeping." Marcia grew up in Boston. She had an accent that Polly had never heard before. Dr. Dan called it a Boston accent.

Polly returned her smile, trying not to feel disappointed that Dr. Dan wasn't awake. She knelt on the rug beside the rocker and in front of the fireplace.

They didn't need the fireplace. The house had one of the new coal-burning furnaces. It made the house more comfortable than heating by parlor stoves or fireplaces.

Too comfortable, her father thought. "The family scatters all over the house now," he said. "Parents hardly know their children these days."

The family didn't need to be together around the stove or fireplace to keep warm in the winter with the coal furnace in the house. Often her father built fires in the fireplace during cool weather, just so the family would spend more time visiting and playing together. Polly liked those times. But there wasn't a fire in the fireplace today, not on a warm day in early May.

"Dr. Dan was out all night helping with people who were injured in the fire," Marcia said in a low voice.

Polly nodded. "Mama said he helped my friend Brita's father."

"Yes, among others. I know he wants to speak with you about Mr. Swenson."

That sounded scary. Polly shifted, spreading her wide skirt carefully over her legs. She glanced up at Marcia, who was smiling down at sleeping Richard. He was almost a year old, not a small baby. "Is he heavy?"

"A little, but I like holding him, even when my arms get tired."

Dr. Dan stirred. He opened his eyes and glanced around slowly.

Polly giggled. He looked like he couldn't figure out where he was. She felt that way when she woke up sometimes.

He rubbed a hand through his black hair, yawned, and sat

up straighter. "Guess I needed a catnap. Sorry to be such poor company."

Marcia just smiled at him. Polly thought Dr. Dan was lucky to be married to such a sweet, pretty lady. She hoped she'd be like Marcia when she grew up.

Marcia stood up with Richard in her arms. "I'll lay Richard down upstairs and leave you two to visit."

When she'd left, Dr. Dan sat forward and patted the big footstool in front of him that matched the overstuffed chair. "Won't you come sit by me?"

Polly sat down on the footstool, facing Dr. Dan. He leaned forward, his elbows on his knees. Polly thought he looked awfully tired. There were circles under his black eyes. His usually crisp white shirt was rumpled.

Polly opened her mouth to speak, but a lump seemed to have formed in her throat. She swallowed hard and tried again. "Marcia says you took care of my friend's father."

He nodded. "Mr. Swenson, yes. He's been badly burned."

"Is he. . .is he going to live?"

"Yes."

Polly heaved a sigh of relief.

"But," Dr. Dan continued, "it will be months before we know how well he will heal. He was burned on one side of his body: his face, shoulder, chest, and arm."

"He's alive. That's the most important thing."

"Yes, but the next few months will be very hard for Brita's family. The healing process will be painful for Mr. Swenson, and he won't be able to work for a while." Dr. Dan took Polly's hands in his big ones and squeezed them lightly. "Your friend will need you more than ever."

"I–I want to tell her how sorry I am, but I don't know what to say to her."

"I know how you feel. Doctors often have to tell people

sad things. There are times when we want to help them but we don't know what to do, even with all our medical training."

Polly bit her bottom lip. "What do you say to them? What are the right words to say that help them when they feel bad?"

He squeezed her hands again. "I've learned there are no words that can take away someone else's pain. The only thing that can help is knowing other people care and love us so much that they wish we didn't have to suffer. What's important is to let Brita know you care about her."

Polly nodded, but inside she was worried. She was more nervous than when she'd had to stand up in front of the entire school for a spelling bee last year. She still didn't know what to say to Brita.

Walter stopped over before Polly and her mother left for the Swenson's house. When Polly told him about Mr. Swenson, he decided to visit the Swenson family with Polly and her mother. Polly was glad he was joining them.

The Swenson house seemed quiet and still. Mrs. Swenson wasn't bustling about as usual. She just rocked quietly in their sparsely furnished parlor. Brita and Per were there, too, dressed in their best clothes.

The house smelled like coffee. Mrs. Swenson offered Polly's mother a cup, and the women went into the kitchen, carrying the stew and pie Polly's mother had made.

Polly looked at Brita and didn't know what to say. She glanced at Walter. He shifted from one foot to the other, his hands stuffed in his trousers' pockets. She could tell he wasn't any more comfortable than she was.

Brita's eyes were red and her face was swollen like she'd been crying. Per looked the same way. They both sat looking at their hands, not saying anything.

Try as she might, Polly couldn't think what to say. *Remember what Dr. Dan said,* she told herself finally. *Just let Brita and Per know we care.*

She cleared her throat, feeling embarrassed. "Um, Dr. Dan told us about your father. I'm sorry he's hurt. I wish. . .I wish he hadn't been hurt. I wish you didn't feel so bad."

She wished she hadn't said anything. It seemed to her everything she said sounded stupid.

Then she heard Walter say, "Me, too. I hope he's better soon."

"Thanks," Per murmured.

Polly had always thought sixteen-year-old Per seemed so grown up. Today he looked young and uncertain of himself.

Brita's lips stretched into a small, quivery smile. "Thank you."

Polly smiled and relaxed a little. Then Brita burst into tears and buried her face in her hands. Per stretched a big arm over her shaking shoulders. Polly thought she saw tears glittering in his eyes, too.

Polly had never felt so uncomfortable. She didn't think she would like her friends to see her crying. When something hurt her inside, like Brita was hurting now, Polly liked to hide it.

She glanced at Walter. He was shifting his feet and looking out the window. She knew he felt as uncomfortable as she did.

Per cleared his throat. "Thanks for coming, you two. Visitors have been stopping by all day to say how sorry they are and ask if they can do anything to help, but they were all friends of Mama and Papa. You're the only friends of ours who have come."

His words made Polly glad she'd come and glad she'd tried to tell them she cared, even if the words she'd said didn't sound like the right ones to her.

Brita sniffed, dug a handkerchief out of her sleeve, and wiped at her eyes. "Papa is in the hospital. The people who work there won't let Per and me see him. They said we're too young."

Polly gasped. "That's awful!"

She couldn't imagine not being able to see her father if he was injured and in the hospital.

"Will he have to stay in the hospital for long?" Walter asked.

"We don't know yet," Per answered.

"Mama says it's a blessing that Per wasn't injured or killed, too," Brita told them.

"I work as a packer on the day shift at the Washburn A mill, you know," Per reminded them. "My shift left at six o'clock last night, an hour and twenty minutes before the explosion. We should be glad the mill didn't explode while the day shifts were working. If it had, hundreds of people would have been killed."

"That doesn't make me feel any better about Papa being hurt," Brita said.

Per patted her shoulder. "We have much to be thankful for, Brita. Remember, Papa is the only man who was at the Washburn A mill when it exploded who wasn't killed."

"I know, but I wish he hadn't been hurt, either."

Polly thought she would feel the same as Brita if it had been her father instead of Mr. Swenson who was injured.

When they were ready to leave, Brita pulled Polly aside. "Would. . .would you pray for my papa?"

Polly gave her a hug. "Of course. I've been praying ever since we saw the fire last night. I'm praying for you, too."

Brita smiled through her tear-filled eyes.

As they walked back to Polly's house, Polly said to Walter, "I'm glad we went over there."

"Me, too."

Chapter 4
The Ruins

Hurrying to meet his baseball club friends after supper, Walter tried to shake the sad feelings that had hung about him after visiting Per and Brita. It would be good to play baseball and get the terrible events of the night before out of his mind for a while.

When he rounded the corner of the wagon shop that stood beside the empty lot where the club practiced, a group of boys was already there. Sherman stood in the middle of them. He was taller than most, and his wavy, reddish-brown hair showed above everyone else's heads.

"My father saw Washburn A explode," Sherman was saying, his green eyes sparkling with excitement.

Walter remembered that Sherman's father worked at a paper mill near the Washburn A flour mill.

The boys were listening to Sherman, spellbound. "Papa says the roof blew hundreds of feet into the air, and then the walls fell down!"

Walter shuddered. He didn't want to think what it must have been like for Brita's father.

"Then the walls of two other mills next to the Washburn A fell in," Sherman continued. "Within minutes the Washburn A was on fire, and then the mills around it, and a nearby grain elevator was on fire from top to bottom."

"How long did the fires burn?" Jack asked.

"The firemen were still pouring water on the flames this morning," Sherman said, looking as though he felt important with all the answers.

Walter was tired of hearing about the fire. "Let's play baseball, guys."

Jack tossed his dirty hair out of his eyes. "Aw, we can play baseball anytime. I say we go to the mill district and see the ruins."

"Yes, let's!" agreed Sherman.

The rest of the kids agreed.

Walter frowned. "Some of the guys aren't here yet. Shouldn't we wait for them?" He glanced around. One of the club members who hadn't shown up yet was Anton. *Where is he?* Walter wondered. He hadn't been at school today, either.

"Why bother?" Jack asked. "We're not going to play ball tonight anyway."

"We were only going to practice," Sherman said. "Besides, tomorrow is Saturday. We can play then." He waved an arm. "Come on, guys!"

The group took off after him down the street toward the mill district.

Walter glanced around the empty lot. He felt guilty not waiting for the rest of the kids.

"Aren't you coming, Fisk?" Sherman called.

Walter swallowed his guilt. Sherman's friendship was important to him. Besides, he really did want to see the ruins. "Coming!" he called, and ran after the group.

The air grew harder to breathe when they got close to the area where the Washburn A building once stood. Smoke still filled the rest of the city, but it was heavier here. Walter's eyes smarted from it. He didn't like the smell of burned wheat that hung in the air, either.

Walter couldn't believe what they saw at the mill district. He saw his friends walking around with their eyes wide and their mouths open, looking stunned. He figured he probably looked the same way.

Even though the smoke was thick, it wasn't as thick as it had been when he, Anton, Polly, and Brita were there the night before. There was a lot more damage than there had been when they left last night, but, of course, the fire had burned a long time after they went home.

Hundreds of people walked around looking at the ruins. Walter, Sherman, and Jack stood at the edge of a crater where the Washburn A had stood until twenty-four hours earlier.

"The tallest, largest building in Minneapolis," Sherman whispered beside him, "gone, just like that!" He snapped his fingers.

The crater was filled with chunks of limestone that used to be walls, timbers that used to be floors and ceilings, and twisted metal that used to be machinery.

"You can't even tell what kind of machinery some of that metal used to be," Walter said. "It's all melted together and twisted about like pretzel bread."

How had Mr. Swenson lived through an explosion and fire

that could do this much damage? Walter wondered. He knew from Dr. Dan that Mr. Swenson wasn't well enough to tell his story yet.

The pile of remains still steamed in places from the water the firemen had poured on it the night before. In other places, embers still smoldered.

The walls of other mills that had burned stood bare against the sky, blackened from the fire. Not a hint remained of the grain elevator Sherman had told them had burned. A machine shop that once stood near Washburn A was as flat as a piece of paper.

Walter, Sherman, and the others walked slowly through the debris that covered the streets. An entire wall had fallen away from the new Washburn B building. The other walls, roof, and floors remained. Some walls sagged under the weight of the flour stored there. "Look."

Sherman looked where Walter pointed to the roof of the Washburn B.

"Looks like something went through the roof there," Walter said, viewing the huge hole.

They wandered farther on. The roof of the woolen mill's shed had caved in. The planing mill that once stood beside the flour mills was nothing but a pile of stone and mangled metal. The Milwaukee and St. Paul Railroad's roundhouse was missing a side.

Walter's father worked for the railroad. "There were twenty freight cars filled with grain that went up in the fire," he told the others.

"Where do the damaged buildings stop?" Jack asked.

Walter wondered the same thing. Everywhere they looked, they only saw more destruction. Besides the eight damaged or destroyed flour mills and the other buildings they'd seen, they came across another machine shop, a cooper shop where barrels were made for the mills, a storehouse, three barns, three houses, and an apartment building that had been hurt in the fire and explosion.

"Oh, no!" Walter stopped in his tracks, not believing what was in front of him.

"What?" Sherman's green eyes looked puzzled.

"This pile of smoking embers in front of us. It used to be Anton's father's sawmill." Walter felt sick inside.

"No wonder he wasn't at school today and didn't come to the Blues ball practice tonight," Sherman said slowly.

Jack cleared his throat as though he was bothered by the thought of their friend's loss, too. "I knew his father owned a sawmill, but I didn't know it was this one or that the fire got it."

Walter tried to ignore the way his stomach was turning over. Two of his good friends had been hurt by the explosion and fire. "I wonder if Anton's father was hurt or k. . .killed."

"I didn't see his name listed in the newspaper as one of the people killed or hurt," Sherman said.

"But the paper said they don't know if everyone's been found," Jack reminded them.

Walter turned and started walking as fast as he could. That wasn't very fast. He had to dodge all the smoldering piles of debris in the street.

"Where are you going?" Sherman asked.

"To see Anton." *His father has to be all right,* he thought. *He just has to.*

Chapter 5
Anton's Troubles

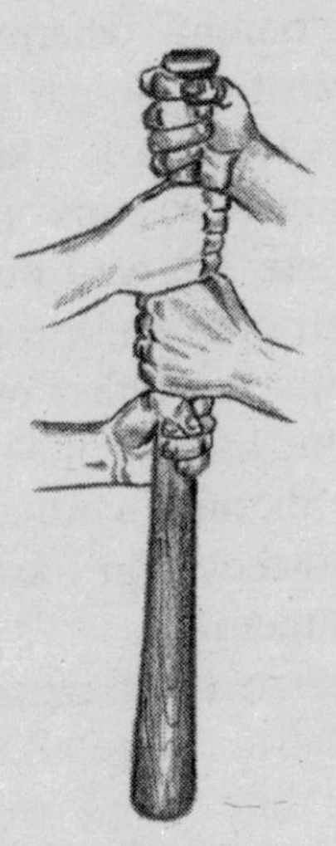

It was dark outside by the time Walter reached Anton's house. No lights shone in the windows. Reluctantly, Walter went home.

"I'm glad you told me about Anton's father's sawmill," Per said the next morning. They had decided to go together to Anton's house. "He might need his friends," Per had said.

Anton was in the backyard chopping wood when they arrived. They all sat on stumps while they talked. Walter was relieved to hear that Anton's father wasn't killed or even hurt.

"That's not so bad, then." Per tried to encourage the sad-looking Anton. "Your father can always rebuild the business with insurance money."

"Maybe."

"What do you mean, maybe?" Per spread his hands wide. "Surely your father had fire insurance."

Anton nodded. "He was talking to the insurance agent yesterday. Whether he gets insurance money depends on which came first, the fire or the explosion."

Walter frowned. "I don't understand."

Thunk! Anton swung his axe and buried the head of it in a nearby stump. "The agent said if the fire was caused by an explosion, then the insurance company doesn't owe *For* anything. If the explosion was caused by a fire, then the fire came first, and the insurance company will pay."

Walter jumped to his feet. "That doesn't sound fair!"

Per nodded. "I agree."

"Well, I guess it is fair, because that's what the contract my *For* signed says. *For* says it's the same for all the companies that were ruined or damaged."

"But there are hundreds of men out of work," Walter protested.

"That's right," Per said. "What will people do if the companies can't afford to rebuild?"

Anton shrugged. "That's what *For* asked. The insurance agent said it wasn't his problem."

"I would have a problem," Per said slowly. "If the Washburn A isn't rebuilt, I won't have a job. Neither will Papa when he's well again."

Things just keep getting worse, Walter thought. He hated feeling so helpless when his friends were facing such terrible problems. Yet there wasn't anything he could do for them.

"The Blues have a baseball match in about an hour,

remember? Can you come, Anton?" he asked. Maybe some baseball would take his friend's mind off his problems for a while.

"I can as soon as I'm done chopping wood for the day."

Per stood up. "I'm going to go to the mill district and see if I can help with the cleanup."

Men were already starting to clean the mess caused by the disaster. Some places, Walter knew, were still smoldering and too hot for people to work in yet.

When Walter and Anton arrived at the empty lot, Walter was surprised to see Polly and Brita there.

"We came to watch," Polly told him while Brita and Anton talked to each other about their families' problems. "We brought a blanket to sit on so we won't get our dresses dirty."

"I don't remember Brita ever watching us practice. It was nice of her to come to our first match."

Polly frowned. "I'm trying to cheer her up a bit. I know she's worried about her father, but I don't like to see her sad *all* the time. She won't play dolls or house or any of the games we usually play."

Walter looked over at Brita and Anton. "I guess we wouldn't feel like playing, either, if our father was hurt as badly as Mr. Swenson."

When he and Polly joined Brita and Anton a minute later, Walter was surprised at the smile on Brita's face. "Guess what, Walter? Polly asked Dr. Dan to let me see Papa at the hospital. He said he will take me to see him, so no one at the hospital can stop me."

"That's great! Can Per go, too?"

"Yes. It will be a couple days before we can see him, though. Dr. Dan says Papa needs his rest right now so he can begin to heal."

Good for Polly, Walter thought. Brita looked happier and

more relaxed than he'd seen her since they first saw the fire from the bridge.

"What's the name of your ball club?" Brita asked.

"The Blues," Walter told her. "When we play against other neighborhood clubs, we wear these blue stockings." He pointed at the stockings that came up to his knees. "Just like real baseball players. I wish we could have shields with the club name on to wear over our shirts like the real ball clubs, but. . ." He shrugged. None of the neighborhood teams had shields.

"What is the name of the club you are playing today?" Polly asked.

"The Mississippis."

Walter secretly liked the other club's name better than the Blues, but he knew that the Mississippi club didn't even wear all the same color socks. They didn't wear anything special to make them look like they were all on the same baseball club.

The other club members started drifting onto the lot. Some came by themselves, others in groups of two or three. Walter was glad to see everyone went over to Anton right away to tell him how sorry they were about his father's sawmill.

"Anton's father gave bats and balls to our club," Walter told Polly and Brita. "Thanks to him, we have better bats than any other kids' baseball club in town."

Brita took the ball he was holding. "This is heavy."

"Anton's father bought that for us, too. It's just like the new balls the National League clubs use. Spalding, of the Chicago club, designed it. The middle is hard rubber. That's wrapped with wool yarn. The outside is stitched horsehide."

Brita made a face and handed the ball back to him. "Horsehide! Yuck!"

Walter laughed. "It's called a dead ball."

Brita and Polly grinned. "We didn't think it was alive," Polly said.

He didn't tell the girls that Mr. Olson's bats and balls were the reason Sherman, Jack, and some of the others treated Anton better than they treated most other Scandinavian children. Because a lot of the Scandinavians didn't speak English very well, some children seemed to think they weren't very smart. Others thought they were better than the Scandinavian students because their families had lived in America longer.

Walter didn't like it when they teased the Scandinavian children. He remembered what it felt like to be the new one in school. He hadn't liked it. He wondered if the Scandinavian children felt that way in America sometimes, with a new language, new places, new customs, and new friends to make.

Anton was his best friend now that Grant had moved to northern Minnesota with his father and brothers. Walter was glad Sherman seldom teased Anton. Sherman was too popular to cross. Walter wouldn't want to have to choose between being friends with Sherman or being friends with Anton.

"Hey, Cap!" Jack yelled from across the lot.

Walter turned around. "I'll be right there."

"Why did he call you 'Cap'?" Brita asked.

"Because I'm the Blues' captain." Walter felt a surge of pride when he answered her.

"They made him captain because he started the club," Polly explained.

Embarrassment pushed away Walter's pride. Maybe what Polly said was partly true, but he liked to think that the other club members also chose him because he was a good player.

Walter's heart raced when he and the Mississippi club captain took turns grabbing the bat handle to see who would choose which club was up to bat first. The Mississippi club captain's hand grasped the end of the bat handle.

"We choose to bat first," the stocky, curly-haired boy said.

From their practices, the Blues' members all knew where

they were to play. Anton jogged to third base. Jack took first. Walter was far out in right field—or as far as he could go on the vacant lot, he thought with a grin. Eric, another Swedish boy, was catcher. Walter knew that some of the club members wished they didn't need any Swedish boys on the club, but if they were good baseballers, they let them play.

Sherman, the club's best player, was the hurler. He pitched the ball to the boys who came up to bat. Sherman was a good hurler, too. He pitched by the same rules as the professional hurlers: from below the waist with the arm perpendicular to the shoulder. He was such a good hurler that he struck out the first three players.

The Blues were in great spirits when they came up to bat. They didn't score the first inning, but they played better than the Mississippi players. At least some of the Blues made it on base.

By the time they made it to the ninth inning, the clubs were tied. Then Sherman struck out a couple players. Two players got hits and made it on base. Another, after nine balls, walked to first.

With all three bases loaded, the pressure was on when the next Mississippi club player came up to bat.

The first pitch was called a ball.

Sherman must be nervous, Walter thought.

The batsman hit the second pitch. The ball went foul.

"Come on, Blues!" Brita's high voice soared out.

"Make him whiff it, Sherman!" Polly yelled.

Hearing Polly use the word "whiff" made Walter laugh. It meant the batsman swung at the ball and missed. *She sounds just like a kranklet at a professional baseball match,* he thought. It was fun for the Blues to have their own kranklets.

The batsman did "whiff" the next three pitches.

"One more strike and he's out, Sherman!" Polly called.

Only one more strike, and we've won the match! Walter thought. He leaned forward, resting his hands on his knees. His heart was beating faster than the hooves of a runaway horse.

Crack!

The bat struck the ball. The ball headed straight toward third base and Anton.

"Get it, Anton!" Walter yelled. He could hear the rest of his team yelling, too.

The Mississippi boys on the bases were running as fast as their legs would go, but that didn't matter if Anton caught the ball.

The ball was going over Anton's head. He leaped for it with both hands in the air.

Whack! Walter heard the ball hit Anton's hands.

It bounced right off his hands onto the ground.

Walter's heart dropped to his stomach.

One of the Mississippi players crossed home base. His club roared.

Anton grabbed the ball and threw it to the catcher. The second Mississippi player crossed home right before the ball reached Eric, who was waiting for it beside home base.

Disappointment flooded Walter. It would be hard to win now, with the Mississippi club two runs ahead of them.

Sherman whiffed the next batsman, putting the Mississippi club out. That didn't help the mood of the Blues players. When they ran in from the field for their last turn at bat, most of the Blues players scowled at Anton.

"Stupid Swede!" Walter heard one of them say.

"Should know better than to let Swedes play baseball," another murmured.

Anton pressed his lips together hard but didn't say anything.

"Are your hands all right?" Walter asked Anton quietly.

"Yah."

"Let me see."

"They aren't hurt," Anton said stubbornly, balling his hands into fists at his sides.

Walter knew Anton's hands had to be stinging badly. *I don't know why he'd be embarrassed about it,* he thought. *Most of the professional baseball players have broken fingers from catching baseballs.* He decided Anton couldn't have broken any fingers, or he wouldn't be able to make fists.

He turned toward Eric to tell him to bat first. Before he could speak, Jack shoved his shoulder.

"You're going to have to move that Swede," Jack demanded. "He can't keep playing third base. It's too important a position."

"I'm leaving him at third," Walter said, turning back to Eric.

Jack walked away, muttering under his breath. Walter breathed a sigh of relief that Jack hadn't said anything more. He was glad Anton hadn't heard Jack.

The Blues didn't score any more runs. They lost to the Mississippis by two points.

"I told you so," Jack said to him later in a low whisper just Walter and Sherman could hear. "It's your Swedish friend's fault we lost."

"Don't forget that Anton's father gives us our balls and bats," Sherman reminded him.

Jack snorted, turned on his heel, and started to leave. He turned back. "Aren't you comin', Sherman?"

Sherman bumped his fist lightly against Walter's shoulder. "It was only our first match. We'll win next time. See ya."

Walter crossed the lot with a heavy heart to where Anton was waiting for him beside the girls. The bats Anton's father had given the team were piled beside him.

"Sorry I lost the match for us, Walter."

The pain in Anton's eyes made Walter feel uncomfortable. "You didn't lose by yourself. It took all of us to lose, the same as it takes all of us to win."

Anton didn't look like he believed him.

Walter gave Anton a big smile. "Come on. Let's go home."

He was glad when Anton and Brita had gone to their own homes and he didn't have to pretend anymore that no one had said anything about Anton's playing.

"At least Brita seemed to enjoy the match," he said to Polly.

"Yes. We're going to go to more of your matches."

He grinned. "Good! I like my club having its own kranks to cheer for us."

Polly grinned back. "We're kranklets, remember? Boys are kranks."

"Right."

Polly puckered her brows together. "I wish girls could play baseball. That would really take Brita's mind off her troubles, at least while she was playing."

Walter burst out laughing. "Who ever heard of girls playing baseball?"

Polly gave him a dirty look and turned in at her front gate. "I should have known better than to cheer for a bunch of stupid boys!"

Picturing girls in ruffled skirts and curls tied back with bows whiffing at balls and diving for balls, Walter chuckled all the way home.

"Look at all the people!" Walter said to Polly after church the next day, putting on the wide-brimmed brown hat he'd removed while inside.

The street was clogged with horse-drawn buggies. Men, women, and children, all in their Sunday best, filled the walk.

It was impossible to walk quickly.

Some of the many strangers pushed their way through the crowd, trying to get wherever they were going as quickly as possible. Polly and Walter's families couldn't even walk together.

Their mothers walked ahead of the rest of the family, chatting. The Terrible Twins, Abe and Judith, were playing tag. Polly's seven-year-old brother, Abe, wove in and out among the people, dodging ladies' and gentlemen's elbows while chasing Judith. Judith was Walter's sister, who was born the same day as Abe.

Polly pressed close to Walter's side on the crowded wooden sidewalk. "I haven't seen this many people since the centennial celebration on the Fourth of July almost two years ago."

"I expect the crowds are from out of town," Polly's father said.

"What are they here for, Uncle Enoch?" Walter asked.

"To see the ruins of the mill fire. Since it's Sunday and most people don't have to work, people are coming from all the countryside and towns around to see the destruction."

"My father has to work," Walter said. "He doesn't like to work on Sundays, because it's the Lord's day, but sometimes he has to anyway. The railroad companies have the railroads run on Sundays, and the engineers like Father have to work when the companies tell them to work."

Enoch nodded. "His engine probably pulled passenger cars filled with people who are visiting the ruins today. Maybe he'll have some exciting stories to tell you when he gets home."

While they walked, Enoch tipped his fancy black stovepipe hat to men they met. He met a lot of people in his position with the bank. Walter noticed that Enoch was walking stiffly and leaning heavier on his black cane than usual. He hoped his uncle's leg wasn't bothering him.

"Don't you like watching all the people in their best clothes on Sundays?" Polly asked. "I love to see all the pretty dresses and bonnets."

Walter rolled his eyes.

"I can't wait until I'm old enough to wear ankle-length gowns with trains." Polly sighed.

Walter snorted. "Trains on dresses are stupid. I don't know how women can even walk with miles of material dragging behind them."

"They wear the longest trains inside, where they don't get in the dirt."

"One day last summer when Mama was having company, she had on her best dress, a green one with a long train with these kind of ruffly things around the edges. She wore it outside to cut some flowers." He started snickering.

"What happened?" Polly asked.

"Thunder, our neighbor's little brown-and-white dog, thought the train was a toy. He grabbed the edge of it in his teeth, growled and growled, and wouldn't let go."

Uncle Enoch chortled, his brown eyes dancing.

"Mama kept turning around in circles, trying to get Thunder to let go. She tugged at the train and even lifted the train right off the ground. Thunder just hung on, dangling off the ground."

Uncle Enoch laughed harder.

Polly darted a suspicious look at Walter. "You made that up, Walter Fisk."

"No I didn't. You can ask Mama. Thunder ruined her dress."

A young man with a soup-strainer mustache pushed past them, knocking Uncle Enoch's cane from his hand. Uncle Enoch stumbled over the cane and lost his balance. His arms waved as he tried to keep from falling. His stovepipe hat tumbled to the ground.

Walter dashed to his side, alarm spreading through his

chest. He put one arm around Uncle Enoch's waist and felt one of his uncle's arms drop on his shoulders.

Polly picked up her father's cane and hat and handed them to him. Her eyes flashed as she watched the back of the young man who hadn't even apologized.

"Thank you," Uncle Enoch said to both of them, leaning on his cane again and adjusting his hat over his curly brown hair. His cheeks were red, and Walter thought he looked embarrassed.

Walter couldn't remember ever seeing Uncle Enoch lose his balance like that before, not since he'd met him when he moved to Minneapolis two years earlier. He knew Uncle Enoch had lost a leg in the War Between the States. Uncle Enoch walked with a different gait than most people with two legs, but he got along very well. He always carried his cane, but then, so did many businessmen, whether they needed a cane or not.

Even though Uncle Enoch only had one leg, Walter had always thought of him as a strong man.

He glanced at Polly. She was staring straight ahead, her green eyes stormy, her lips set in a firm line. He knew she was more than angry. She was hurting inside because she couldn't make her father the same as most men.

Suddenly he felt small and helpless. So many of his friends had fathers who were hurting in one way or another, and none of them could help their fathers. Brita's father was still in the hospital. Anton's father's sawmill had burned. And now he saw how Polly wished she could make things better for her father.

Sometimes, he thought, *being young is awfully tough.*

Chapter 6
The Factory

After dinner, Walter and Anton headed for the ruins again. It was exciting to be among the crowd. The police were trying to keep order. They'd stretched ropes around the ruins to keep people at a safe distance, but some—mainly boys and young men—dodged under the ropes for a closer look.

Firemen were still pouring water on some of the burned buildings where embers continued to smolder. Steam hissed from them.

"What is that awful odor?" Walter heard one woman ask

the man beside her. "Not the smoke, but that other smell."

"Burning wheat," Walter told her. He was used to that smell now. It had filled the air ever since the explosion and fire on Thursday.

Even though it was Sunday, workmen were digging through the ruins. It was important to the city that things be cleaned up as soon as possible and the mills and other businesses rebuilt. Many people were out of work. Flour was one of the main ways people made money in Minneapolis.

It seemed to Walter the men were trying to do more than clean up the debris. "What are they looking for?" he asked a man he recognized from his neighborhood.

"Safes, with the companies' records telling who owes them money and who they owe money."

"Oh."

The man wiped a hand over his mustache and short beard. "And they're looking for bodies, too. They haven't yet found all the people who were killed in the explosion. They did find one more body this morning. Course, it was burned so bad that no one could tell who it was."

Walter felt his stomach turn over, and his face turned green. "Let's go," he said to Anton.

Anton must not have wanted to see anything gruesome either, Walter decided, for he turned and walked beside Walter and away from the ruins without a word.

"Have you heard whether the insurance company will pay for your father to rebuild his sawmill?" Walter asked.

"Not yet. *For* says a jury is going to decide whether the explosion or fire came first. After that, we will know about the insurance."

"That must be tough."

"*For* says it's worse for the men who worked for him. At least insurance money might help him rebuild. There is no insurance to pay men who are put out of work because of the fire. Those men need the money they earn to pay for their families' housing and food."

Walter nodded. "The families of the men who were killed need help, too. Some of them belong to groups like the Knights of Pythias, who help each other in bad times. Father says everyone who belongs to the group gives a little money each year. The money is put together in something called a death fund. Then if one of the men in their group is killed, some of this money is given to the man's wife and children. Some of the widows of the men killed in the mill fire received a thousand dollars from death funds!"

"Yah," Anton agreed, "but the families of the men who didn't belong to a group like that don't receive any money."

They quietly walked along together for a few minutes, dodging people and horses and carriages. Walter didn't know how the horses and carriages could get through the streets. Close to the ruins, twisted metal, broken glass, chunks of limestone from buildings' walls, and pieces of timber covered everything. Soot was everywhere and covered the boys' shoes with gray dust.

Walter couldn't get the families of the men who were killed out of his mind. "Some organizations are putting on plays or selling baked goods to raise money for the widows and orphans. That will help some, I suppose," he said to Anton.

"My father has given some money to each of the men who work for him," Anton said quietly, "to help them until the sawmill is rebuilt."

"Like a loan that they can repay when they have their jobs back?"

"No." Anton pushed his wavy, dark blond hair out of his eyes. "He just gave it to them."

Walter smiled. He always smiled when Anton said "just."

Like so many Scandinavians Walter had met, Anton pronounced the word "yoost." No matter how many times Walter corrected him, Anton couldn't seem to remember how to pronounce the word correctly. Walter had finally given up trying to change him.

"That was really nice of your father," Walter said. "Not everyone would give their employees money like that."

"*For* told me once that he always asks himself, 'What would Jesus do?' Sometimes he says it's hard to know the answer, and you have to do what you think is best and hope that is what Jesus wants you to do." Anton kicked at a pebble. "I think he asked himself, 'If Jesus owned my sawmill, what would He do for the men who are out of work?' "

Walter thought Anton's father probably found the right answer this time.

A week and a half later, Polly hurried over to Brita's house after supper. She found Brita in the kitchen. Her cheeks were bright red from stirring a stew that simmered on the black woodstove.

"Would you like to work on the shields tonight?" Polly asked. "We haven't much homework, so we have time to sew."

After watching the Blues play, Brita had come up with the idea of making the players shields to wear over their shirts, like Walter had said he wanted. Polly thought it was a great idea. They'd spent hours working on them together, and Polly thought it had helped take Brita's mind off her father.

"You haven't told Walter about the shields yet, have you?" Brita asked.

Polly's curls bounced off the shoulders of her yellow-and-red school dress as she shook her head. "No. It's still our surprise. Only Mother knows, because she gave us the material and thread."

"Good." Brita took some bowls from the open cupboard

and set them on the red-and-white checked cloth that covered the white wooden table in the kitchen. "I don't think I can work on them tonight." She hesitated, tugging gently at one corner of the tablecloth as though straightening it, though it didn't look crooked to Polly.

"Why?"

"I–I don't think I will have time to help you finish the shields for a long time."

Something is wrong, Polly thought. She could feel something tightening and turning inside her stomach. "I don't understand."

"Mama started a job three days ago, on Monday."

Polly stared at her. They both had friends whose mothers worked, but not many. Most of the mothers they knew stayed home and took care of their families and homes. Some mothers whose husbands were dead ran boarding houses, or they took in sewing, but usually they worked in their own houses. Single ladies often worked outside the home, but not after they married. Sometimes mothers in poor families had to work. But why Mrs. Swenson? And why hadn't Brita told her? Was she ashamed that her mother was working?

Polly watched Brita take a loaf of bread from the wooden pie safe with its punched tin doors. She set it on a breadboard on the table and began slicing the bread.

"Where is your mother working?" Polly got up the courage to ask.

"She's a seamstress."

"That's not so bad. That's just sewing, like our mothers do for us all the time, only it's for other people. Is she working here, at your home?"

"No. She's working at a shirt factory. She has to start early in the morning and work until six in the evening."

Polly frowned. "When will she do her housework?"

Brita rubbed her hands down the front of the apron that

covered most of her brown housedress. "I have to help. I have to do a lot more chores. That's why I won't have time to help you finish the baseball shields for Walter's club. I'm sorry."

"That's all right. I can finish them myself, but it was more fun doing them together."

Brita smiled.

The back door banged open, letting in the fresh smell of new spring grass and leaves to blend with the wood smoke from the stove and the meat and bay leaf of the simmering stew. Per came in on the spring breeze that lifted the edge of the tablecloth.

Brita crossed her arms in front of her. "Don't you dare walk across my clean floor, Per Swenson. Not in those filthy clothes."

Polly giggled. Brita sounded just like Mrs. Swenson. But Per *was* covered from head to toe in gray soot. He smelled like soot, too, even from across the wide kitchen. "What have you been doing?" she asked.

Per took off his hat and slapped it. Dust went everywhere.

"Pe-e-er!"

He ignored Brita's protest. "I got a job helping clean up the rubble at the ruins. It doesn't pay well, but until the mills are rebuilt, I won't have my regular job back."

Brita interrupted. "Are you going to shake that soot off outside or not?"

Per gave her a disgusted look. "If it hasn't fallen off on the walk home, what makes you think I can shake it off now?"

"Why don't you brush it off with a broom?" Polly suggested.

Brita and Per both thought that was a good idea. Brita got the straw broom from the pantry, and the three of them went outside. Since Per couldn't very well brush himself off with the long-handled broom, Brita did it for him. Soon the ground around Per was surrounded by a black circle.

Brita sighed. "You're still not clean. Why don't I bring you clean clothes, and you can change in the shed?"

Reluctantly, Per agreed.

"I've used all the wood you had split for the kitchen stove," Brita told him, "but if you'll bring me more after you've changed, I'll heat water for you so you can clean yourself up."

Polly fidgeted with the sides of her dress as she followed Brita inside. It was strange hearing Brita talk like a grown-up woman, like she was running the house instead of her mother.

When they were back in the warm kitchen, Polly said, "At least it's a good thing that your mother and Per have jobs. You won't have to worry about money until your father can work again."

Brita sprinkled flour on the small, square wooden work-table. Then she took sticky biscuit dough from an earthenware bowl and began rolling it out with a wooden rolling pin. "I guess you don't know very much about how much money people make at their jobs, do you?"

Polly selected forks, spoons, and knives for the table. She didn't like standing around watching Brita work and not helping. "What do you mean?"

"Well, Per doesn't make very much at his job because he's young and because you don't have to know very much to clean up messes like that."

"But your mother has to know how to be a good seamstress for her job. She should make more money."

Brita shook her head. "She doesn't make any more than Per. Mama told me that women never make as much money as men for the same work. That's why some people like to hire women—because they do the same work for so much less money."

Polly stared at Brita, her hands filled with tableware. "That's not fair!"

Brita shrugged. Her blond braids hung over her shoulders

and over the front of her apron. Cheerful red ribbons that matched the little flowers in her brown dress were tied at the bottom of her braids and added a bright note to her outfit. Polly thought nothing else seemed very happy in this house tonight.

"I guess if life was fair," Brita said slowly, "Papa wouldn't have been hurt. He's a good man. He didn't deserve to be hurt like that."

"No, he didn't." Polly felt uncomfortable. She wished she could think of something to say that would make Brita feel better.

She watched while Brita placed a pan of biscuits in the oven.

"Did Dr. Dan let you see your father yet?"

Polly saw tears glint in Brita's eyes. "Yes," Brita said. "Papa's head and part of his face and his shoulder and arm were all covered in white bandages. He couldn't talk very well. Dr. Dan said that was because of the bandages and the burns on his face."

"I'm sure he was glad to see you."

Brita nodded, her braid bows dancing. "Dr. Dan is going to teach Mama how to care for Papa's wounds and change his bandages so Papa can stay at home. That way we won't have to pay as many hospital bills."

The back door swung open, and Mrs. Swenson came inside. Over one arm was a pile of shirts. From her elbow swung a small tin pail like those in which men carried their lunch to and from work every day. Per followed her with a load of wood, which he dumped noisily into the box beside the cookstove.

"Why, hello, Polly," Mrs. Swenson said with a smile.

"Hello." Polly thought Mrs. Swenson looked awfully tired. There were big dark circles beneath her eyes, and her shoulders seemed to slump beneath the simple white blouse she wore. "Are those some of the shirts you sewed?"

Mrs. Swenson laid the shirts over the back of a chair beside the kitchen table. "Yes. I need to sew the buttons on tonight and bring the shirts back to work in the morning."

"Oh." Polly thought it was awful that Mrs. Swenson had to bring work home with her. Didn't her employer know that married ladies had lots of other work to do at home?

Mrs. Swenson lifted the lid of the cast-iron kettle, closed her eyes, and sniffed. "Mmmm. This stew smells good." She smiled at Brita. "It looks like you've done a fine job preparing supper tonight."

Brita beamed.

Per brushed wood chips from the arms of his blue cotton shirt into the wood box. "I met a couple professors at the ruins today, Mama. Their names are Professor Peck and Professor Peckham. They teach physics and chemistry at the University of Minnesota."

Mrs. Swenson stared at him in surprise. "And what would professors be doing in the ruins?"

"Looking for clues. They're trying to find out whether the explosion or fire came first and what caused them. They want to talk to Papa."

"What can he tell them?" she asked.

Per shrugged. "I don't know, but he was there before the fire and explosion. Everyone else who was in Washburn A at the time was killed. Papa is one of the expert millers, so he can tell them about any other fires at the mill in the past."

Mrs. Swenson tied a large apron over her blouse and skirt. "What do two professors want to know about the explosion?"

"They're supposed to report to the jury that is to decide for the insurance companies whether the fire or explosion came first," Per answered.

"I hope your papa's answers to the professors' questions

make the insurance companies pay, so the mills can be rebuilt soon," Mrs. Swenson said with a sharp nod of her head.

Polly edged toward the door. "Well, I guess I'd better go home. I've lots to do tonight."

Sitting in the family living room later, she carefully stitched the word "Blues" across the front of a shield in blue thread. She looked up and glanced about at her family.

Her mother was darning socks and chatting quietly with Marcia, who was hemming a tiny shirt for Richard. Dr. Dan was working at the hospital.

Abe was on the floor with Richard. Abe would run his toy railroad engine past Richard, and Richard would squeal while trying to grab it.

Her father sat in his comfortable, overstuffed chair with the newspaper on his lap, as usual. His cane rested beside the chair, also as usual.

It was like this at Polly's house almost every night.

Brita's family used to be like this, too, she thought. Now Brita's father was in the hospital, her mother was sewing buttons on someone else's shirts instead of the family's shirts, and Brita was doing her mother's chores.

Polly made the last stitch on the "s" at the end of "Blues" and tied a knot at the back of the shield. Instead of the joy she'd felt the last few days working on the shields with Brita, her chest was filled with sadness.

Chapter 7

The Experiment

"I hate washing clothes." Brita grabbed the plunger's wooden handle and pushed it to the bottom of the tub of hot water filled with clothes. Water sloshed over the sides and onto the ground in her backyard.

"I feel the same way." Polly pushed a wooden clothespin over one of Per's freshly washed work shirts.

"At least it's more fun when you help," Brita lifted another shirt out of the hot, soapy water with the handle of the plunger and dropped the shirt into a large tub of clean water to rinse it.

Other than at school, the only way I get to see Brita anymore is if I help with her chores, Polly thought.

Polly pushed at her rolled-up sleeves and dunked the shirt in the clean water a few times to get out the soap. Then she stuck one end of the shirt between the rollers of the wringer and turned the crank. "Oof!" It was hard to turn. The shirt moved slowly through the rollers. Water squeezed out of it and back into the tub. The shirt dropped into a wicker basket on the ground below the tub.

Brita dumped another shirt into Polly's rinse water. "I'm glad you brought your mother's new wringer, Polly. That's a lot easier than wringing clothes out by hand."

Polly flapped her hand up and down and grinned. "Yes, but it still makes my arm tired."

"Want to trade for a while?"

"All right."

Polly took the plunger. When she looked down at the wash water, she made a face. "Yuck. I think it's time to change the water. This water is almost black."

Brita sighed so loud that it made Polly laugh. She brushed back the brown hair that was curling about her sweaty face.

"Per's clothes get so dirty working at the ruins," Brita complained. "I told Mama we shouldn't even bother to wash them. They won't stay clean for five minutes after he wears them to work."

"It must feel terrible to put on filthy clothes in the morning, though."

Brita shook her head. "Washing them doesn't seem to help much. They'll never look like new again."

Polly laughed. Brita was right. "Come on, help me dump this water out."

Together they turned the tub on edge. The water poured out, turning the ground beneath it to mud.

Polly grinned. "Good thing we decided to work barefooted."

They carried the tub to a dry part of the yard. Polly took a knife and shaved slivers of brown soap into the tub. Then the girls went inside to get kettles of water.

There were four kettles on the stove, but each was so heavy that it took both girls to carry one at a time. The handles of the kettles were hot, and the girls had to use hot pads while they carried the kettles into the yard. Polly held her breath almost the whole way, trying hard not to spill the water. They had to make four trips to fill the tub.

"I'd better put more water on to heat," Brita said.

"But we're almost done. We've only another of Per's shirts and two pair of his trousers to wash."

"We might need clean rinse water again, though."

Polly dropped another shirt into the tub. Steam rose from the water. While she plunged the shirt to the bottom of the tub again and again, she could hear Brita pumping water into the kettles at the kitchen sink. It was the twentieth of May, and the kitchen windows and door were open to help keep the house cool while the water heated.

It's been almost three weeks since the big fire, she thought, *and there's still lots to clean up at the ruins.*

The rope Mrs. Swenson had strung between trees and the shed for a clothesline sagged with the clothes Polly and Brita had washed. As always, they'd started with the least dirty clothes, so the water wouldn't need to be changed as often.

They were hanging the last of Per's trousers on the line when he walked into the yard.

Polly looked at him and laughed. "I thought you'd be wearing clothes as disgustingly dirty as the ones we just washed."

He grinned. "I didn't work at the ruins today. I was excused by the boss to help Professor Peck put on a demonstration for the jury."

"How could *you* help a professor?"

"I stood on a box."

Polly and Brita looked at each other, then back at Per. Polly crossed her arms over her work apron. Brita did the same. "You did *what*?" Polly asked, raising her eyebrows.

Per dropped down on the back steps. "I stood on a box."

"That's what I thought you said." Polly squinted at him. "Why?"

"Because Professor Peck asked me to."

"Didn't you feel stupid, standing on a box in front of all those men in the jury?" Brita asked.

"I didn't stand on it long."

"Good." Brita looked at Polly and smiled.

"Not long at all," he continued. "Only until I was blown off."

"What?"

"What?"

"I said—"

"We heard what you said." Polly held up her hands, palms toward Per. "Maybe you should start at the beginning."

Per pushed his wide-brimmed hat with its round crown back on his head until his blond hair showed above his wide forehead. "Well, Professor Peck was trying to show the jury that the dust and other things made when flour is ground in a mill won't explode easily, remember?"

Polly and Brita nodded.

"First, he took a board and placed nine different mill dusts and grain meal on it. Then he passed the flame of a Bunsen burner over them."

"Did they explode?" Brita asked.

"No. They each burned for a couple seconds, but that's all. Then he took a bellows and blew each of the meals and dusts into the air over a flame."

"What happened?"

"They almost exploded into flame."

Brita frowned. "I don't understand. Is that important?"

"Not by itself," Per explained. "He had to do more demonstrations to convince the jury that a fire caused the explosion."

Polly grinned. "Let me guess. He did that by making you stand on a box."

"Right."

"I was teasing."

"You were still right, Polly," Per said with a smile. "Professor Peck took an uncovered, lighted kerosene lamp and placed it in the wooden box. Then he put a heavy, loose cover over it."

"And you stood on it."

"Right, Brita. Me and another man."

"Did the box catch on fire from the lamp?" Polly asked.

"No. Let me finish." Per leaned forward, his blue eyes shining. "Professor Peck took some of the dust like that he'd burned in the first demonstration and used the bellows to blow it beneath the loose cover and into the box with the lighted lamp. The dust exploded."

Polly gasped.

Brita gasped, too, and clutched her hands to her chest. "It exploded with you on top of the box?"

Per laughed. "Yes and no. When it exploded, the top of the box was lifted, and I and the other man fell off. A sheet of flame shot out of the box for several feet in every direction."

Polly could feel her heart beating fast and hard against her ribs. "You could have been badly hurt!"

Brita just stared at him.

Per shrugged, still smiling. "I wasn't afraid. I trusted Professor Peck. He had told me and the other man on the box that the explosion wouldn't be strong enough to hurt us."

"I think it sounds like a stupid thing to do, Per Swenson," Brita said, yanking off her damp work apron. "Honestly, standing on a box and letting someone almost blow you up! What were you thinking?"

"You don't understand," he said patiently. "What we did was important. The demonstrations convinced the jury that the dust had to catch on fire to cause the explosion that destroyed Washburn A and the nearby mills."

"So?" Brita glared at him.

"So that means the explosion didn't cause the fire. The fire caused the explosion. And that means the insurance companies have to help pay to rebuild the flour mills."

"Oh! That's wonderful!" Brita threw her arms around Per's neck.

"That *is* wonderful," Polly agreed. "Was that all the professor had to do to prove it to the jury?"

"Well, he did a few other demonstrations, but those were the most important ones. When he was done, Professor Peckham showed the jury how a piece of gravel or metal that was in the feed being ground by the millstones could cause a spark that would make the dust in the mill explode."

"Is there usually a lot of dust in the mills?" Polly asked.

Per nodded. "Papa and the other millers wore sponges over their mouths and noses when they worked so they could breathe better."

"That sounds awful!"

"There's no proof that what the professors showed could happen is what actually happened at Washburn A," Per went on, "but I think the jury believes it probably did happen that way. I think what Papa told the professors helped, too."

"What was that?" Brita asked.

"He explained to them how the dust and hot air from the grinding moved through the mill to the dust house at the side of the mill. That helped Professor Peckham know where the fire might have started."

Brita smiled widely.

Polly smiled back at her. She knew Brita was proud of her father and Per.

"I still think you were brave to let Professor Peck explode a box right under your feet," Brita told Per.

Per's cheeks turned bright red, but he gave her a big smile.

CHAPTER 8

Trouble for the Blues

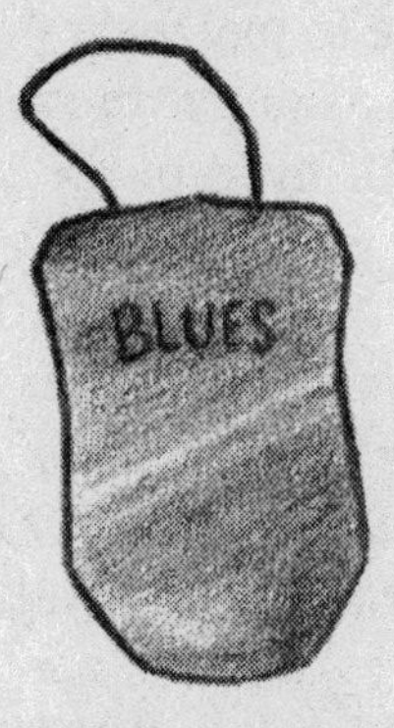

Walter didn't smile that evening when Polly told him that the insurance companies would probably be helping to pay for the buildings that were destroyed.

"It won't help Anton Olson's father," Walter told her.

"Why not?"

"His insurance agent told him today that the insurance company doesn't have enough money to pay all the claims that have been made for this fire."

Polly stared at him. "What is he going to do?"

"He can't afford to rebuild without the insurance. Anton says he's going to sell their house and use the money to pay his employees the wages he owed them and the sawmill's creditors."

"That's awful!"

"One of the flour mill owners has already offered to buy the land where the sawmill stood. Anton thinks Mr. Olson will sell that, too."

Dread spread through Polly's chest like a small river. "Are all the businesses and houses that burned insured by the same company? Won't anyone be able to rebuild?"

Walter shook his head. "The businesses were insured by lots of different insurance companies. Most of the insurance companies will be able to pay what they owe." He sighed and ran a hand through his straight brown hair. "The jury's decision is a good thing for most of the mills. They'll be able to start rebuilding soon, and men can go back to work. I wish things were better for Anton's father, though."

"I do, too," Polly said quietly. Her chest filled with sadness again. *It seems like the sadness never goes away for long anymore,* she thought. *It must be worse for Brita and Per and Anton.*

"Does your club have a baseball match next Saturday?" she asked.

"Yes, but I don't think it will cheer Anton up very much."

Maybe, if she worked very hard, she could finish the shields by Saturday. The shields might make Anton and Walter a *little* happier.

Polly stayed up late every night that week. After the rest of the family was in bed, she lit the lamp on her bedside table and stitched until she couldn't stay awake any longer. She finished the last shield Friday night, well after midnight.

She opened the drawer in the cupboard in her room and set the shield on top of the others. Her fingers played across the blue stitching of the word "Blues" on the top shield. A smile spread across her face and a warm feeling filled her heart as she crawled between the sheets.

Even though she'd been up late, Polly awoke early the next

morning. The sun shone in through the lace curtains. She dressed hurriedly in a cheerful yellow dress with tiny blue flowers on it. The color was a little faded, as it was an old dress she no longer wore to school, but she liked the dress anyway. Yellow was one of her favorite colors. Then she wrapped the shields in a piece of brown wrapping paper and tied the package with twine. She didn't want Walter seeing the shields before they arrived at the lot where the match would be played.

"Can I make some cookies this morning?" she asked her mother over breakfast.

"I think it's a good idea to get the baking done this morning, before the day turns too warm to use the stove," Mama said, "but I think we need bread more than cookies. I already have the bread dough rising."

"I'd rather have cookies." Abe stuck a spoonful of oatmeal into his mouth.

Mama brushed back a lock of red hair that had escaped the bun at the back of her neck. She smiled at Abe. "You'd always rather have sweets, but your muscles need bread."

"Please, Mama," Polly begged. "I want to bring cookies to Walter's baseball match today. I thought the boys on the team would like them."

"If you bake the bread first and there's still time, you can bake the cookies later."

"Thank you, Mama! I have the sh. . ." she glanced at Abe, who was watching her with his brown eyes wide with curiosity. "I have the surprises ready for the club, too."

"How nice! Can I see them?"

"You have a surprise for Walter's baseball club?" Abe asked.

Polly groaned. "Do all little brothers' ears grow when they hear the word 'surprise'?"

Abe put both hands over his ears. "My ears aren't growing."

Mama laughed. Polly only shook her head.

"What's the surprise?" Abe asked, digging his spoon into the bowl of oatmeal again.

"Surprise is another word for secret," Polly told him. "And secrets are things you don't want little brothers to find out."

"Why?"

"Because they tell everything they know."

"Now, Polly, you're exaggerating," their mother protested softly.

"Yes." Abe nodded firmly. "You're 'zaggeratin', Polly." His brows met above his nose. "What's 'zaggeratin' mean?" he asked his mother.

"It means a person is making something bigger than it really is."

"Oh." His eyes grew big and he gave a funny grin. "Are you making *me* bigger, Polly?"

Mama giggled.

Polly groaned again.

"Can I help you make cookies?" Abe asked around a spoonful of oatmeal.

"Don't talk with your mouth full," Mama said. "Yes, you can help make cookies."

"Mother!"

"Now, Polly, it won't hurt to let him help."

"But he eats all the cookie dough. We won't have enough cookies left to take to the match."

"You're exaggerating again."

"Yes." Abe grinned, and oatmeal dripped down his chin. "You're 'zaggeratin' again."

Polly covered her face with her hand. "Brothers!"

He did leave enough dough for Polly to make a couple dozen sugar cookies. She wrapped them in a clean white linen dish towel and tied the ends together.

By the time she was ready to leave for the match, Walter's sister, Judith, was at their house.

"Why don't you take Judith and Abe to the baseball match with you?" Mrs. Stevenson asked.

"Yes!" Abe yelled. "We want to go, don't we, Judith?"

"Yes!"

Polly closed her eyes. "Must I, Mother?"

"It will be fun for them, and they won't be too much bother."

The Terrible Twins are always a bother, she thought, but she knew better than to say so. "You'll have to help me carry things," she told Abe and Judith.

She had Abe carry the blanket and handed Judith the dish towel filled with cookies.

"*I* want to carry the cookies," Abe said, reaching for them.

Polly grabbed his hand. "If you carry them, there won't be any left when we get to the lot. You'll eat them all."

She didn't dare let him carry the package of shields, either. He'd be sure to tear it open to see what was in it and spoil her surprise.

When they reached the baseball lot, Walter and Anton gave them wide smiles. "You brought more kranks and kranklets to cheer for us!" Anton said.

Abe and Judith looked at each other and grinned. Polly noticed there was a black hole in Judith's smile where she'd lost one of her baby teeth.

Walter told the twins where to spread the blanket. While they were busy doing that, she held out her package to Walter. "This is for the Blues."

Walter's brow puckered in a puzzled look, but he took the package and untied the string. Anton watched from beside him.

"Shields!" Walter's smile seemed to reach from ear to ear. "How did you ever. . .where. . . ?"

Polly's heart swelled with happiness. She'd wanted so

much for him to like the shields! "Brita and I made them. It was Brita's idea." She wished Brita could be here to see Walter and Anton's smiling faces.

Anton picked one up and held it in front of his shirt. "How's it look?"

"Like a professional baseballer's outfit," Walter said.

"We didn't think we could do buttonholes, like on the professional shields," Polly said apologetically, "so we made ties on the top and bottom instead. You can tie them under your shirt collar and around your back."

"That will work swell." Walter handed her back the package and tied one on right away. Anton tied his on, too. They looked at each other and grinned.

Anton laughed. "Wait until the other club sees us dressed like this today. All the clubs are going to want shields now."

Abe grabbed up a shield and started tying it around his neck. Polly stamped her foot, sending up a small cloud of dust. "Take that off right now, Abraham Stevenson. We only made enough for the club."

Abe kept trying to tie it behind his head. "I want to be on the Blues."

"You're too young," Walter said. "Maybe next year."

Abe threw the shield on the ground, stuck out his bottom lip, and stalked back to the blanket where Judith was sitting.

When the rest of the Blues arrived, Walter and Anton handed out the shields.

Some of Blues had heard that Anton's father was selling their house and couldn't afford to rebuild his business. They told him they were sorry.

"Too bad about your father's business," Jack said, tossing his hair back out of eyes. "I guess he won't be buying us any more bats and balls, huh?"

"No, I guess not." Anton kicked at a clump of weeds.

Walter dug an elbow into Jack's side.

"Oof! What was that for?"

Walter just scowled at him.

I wish I were a boy, Polly thought. *I'd sock that old Jack Griggs right in his pug nose.*

Sherman put a hand on Anton's shoulder. "Tough luck. I hope things get better for you and your family soon."

Anton thanked him, then handed him a shield. "Polly and Brita made these for us."

"These are great!" Sherman's green eyes sparkled with his smile. "Thanks, Polly."

Polly felt her cheeks grow warm with a blush. Sherman was so cute and so popular! She was especially glad he liked the shields.

"Polly!" Judith's voice rose over the boys' chatter as they prepared to play. "Abe is eating the cookies!"

"Abe! Stop that!" She turned to Sherman and Walter. "I brought cookies for the Blues, too."

Sherman grinned. "You're the best kranklet we ever had. I hope you come to more of our matches."

Her stomach felt like grasshoppers were jumping in it when she hurried back to the blanket to rescue the cookies. She knew Sherman was only being friendly, like he would be to any of the club members' sisters. Still, it felt good to have someone so popular say such nice things to her.

"Where did you get those terrific shields?" she heard the other club's captain asked Walter.

"My cousin and her friend made them," Walter told him, pointing to her.

"I should ask my sisters if they'll make our club some. Course, they'd have to say North Stars instead of Blues. We named our club North Stars 'cause Minnesota is the North Star State."

Polly thought her day couldn't get much better.

It was fun to watch the match with Abe and Judith. The Terrible Twins yelled until their voices sounded scratchy. They jumped up and down. They clapped and screamed "Hurrah!" whenever one of the Blues made a hit or a catch. And they booed the North Stars.

"You guys make great kranks," Sherman told them between the eighth and ninth innings. "We Blues should get all our brothers and sisters to come to the matches and cheer us on."

"The Blues are playing pretty well," Polly said shyly.

"So are the North Stars. They're ahead seven to six." He jogged off to take his place in the middle of the diamond and pitch.

Sherman was pitching well. On his first three pitches, the batsman made three strikes.

"How many strikes until he's out?" Judith asked for the tenth time.

"Four," Polly and Abe said at the same time.

Whack! The batsman hit the ball far into the field where Walter was playing.

"Catch it, Walter!" Polly yelled.

"Catch it, Walter!" Abe and Judith screamed.

When Walter caught it, Abe and Judith grabbed hands and jumped around in a circle, yelling at the tops of their lungs.

The next batsman hit the ball, too. This one didn't go as far. Jack put the North Star player out at first base.

The next two batsmen made it on base.

With one North Star on second and another on third, the next batsman knocked the ball straight down the line toward Anton.

The North Star players on base started running.

"Get it, Anton!" Polly could hardly hear herself scream over Abe and Judith's voices.

Anton lunged for the ball.

Missed.

Another Blues player caught up the ball and tossed it to Eric, the catcher, but not before two of the North Star players raced over the flour sack that marked home base.

Sherman struck the next North Star out, but that didn't cheer up the Blues much.

When the Blues came in from the field, Jack jerked his head toward third base, where Anton had been playing. "That stupid Swede couldn't catch the croup, let alone a baseball!"

"He didn't miss the ball because he's Swedish, *dum kopf.*" Eric, another Swede, glared at Jack.

"That's right," Walter agreed. "Anyone can make a mistake or miss a ball. Forget it." He leaned down and made sure the rocks that held the flour sack for home plate were in place. "Let's get back to playing and beat these North Stars."

Sherman was the first to bat. He hit a long ball into the field and made it to second base.

Eric was up next. He struck out.

"Don't know why you Swedes even bother to try to play baseball," Jack said to Eric on his way to bat.

I hope that awful Jack Griggs strikes out, too, Polly thought, *even if it means the Blues lose.*

Jack didn't strike out. He hit the ball solid and raced toward first base. Before he made it, the ball was caught by a boy in right field.

Polly cheered.

Jack glared at her.

She smiled sweetly and shrugged her shoulders.

Walter was the next batsman.

"Whack it, Walter!" Polly cried.

"Hit it! Hit it!" Abe and Judith yelled.

Crack!

Walter hit the ball out of the lot. His clubmates leaped up and down, smacking each other on the back, while Sherman ran home from second base and Walter ran around the whole diamond, grinning the entire time.

Polly grabbed Abe's and Judith's hands. "We only need one more run to tie! I mean, the Blues only need one more run to tie the North Stars!"

Anton was the next player up to bat.

Whiff! Whiff! Whiff! Whiff! Four strikes!

Anton was out, and so were the Blues.

The North Stars were cheering, celebrating their win. The Blues stood about with long faces, watching the North Stars or staring at the ground.

Anton tossed down his bat and headed across the field. Walter ran after him. They were close enough to where Polly sat that she could hear them talk.

"Hey, aren't you going to wait and walk home together, Anton?"

Anton looked at the ground instead of at Walter. "No, I've got to be getting home. I'm sorry I struck out."

Walter shrugged. "Everyone strikes out sometimes."

"See you later."

Walter stared after Anton's back for a minute, then turned and went back to where the rest of the Blues were standing. Polly followed him with her towel full of cookies.

She started handing out cookies to the Blues players.

"You need to replace Anton at third base," Jack said to Walter. "That stupid Swede can't play worth a penny."

"I'm not moving him," Walter said quietly.

"We need a *good* player at third," Jack insisted.

"What if Anton gets mad if Walter takes him off third base?" asked a player Polly didn't know. "Then Anton's dad might not give us bats and balls anymore."

"He can't give us bats and balls anyway," Jack told him. "Didn't you hear? Anton's father is broke. There's no reason we need to keep him on the club anymore when he's such a bad player. I say we get rid of him."

His cruel words surprised Polly so much that she dropped a cookie on the ground. She glanced at Walter. Surely he wouldn't listen to Jack and turn against his friend Anton!

CHAPTER 9

Bad News

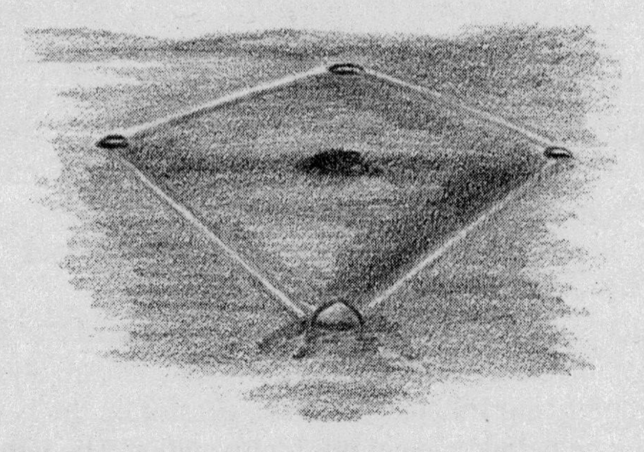

Fury filled Walter until his chest hurt from it. He took a deep breath, trying to keep his temper. "I'm the captain. I say Anton plays third base, and that's that."

"It's all Anton's fault we lost," Jack said.

"Yeah!"

"That's right!"

"We need a *good* player at third base, like Jack said, not a lousy Swede."

Walter couldn't believe most of the other club members were agreeing with Jack. He held up both his hands. "Stop it, all of you! It's not Anton's fault we lost. If you wouldn't have all been busy blaming him for missing that ball at third, you probably would have played better when we were up to bat last time." He pointed a finger at Jack. "*You* shouldn't have hit the ball right to the outfielder. You made an out with that hit, the same as Anton made an out by striking out."

Jack shoved Walter's hand aside. "At least I hit the ball. That's more than that stupid Swede did. I didn't let the ball past me and let two North Stars make it to home base."

Eric loomed at Walter's shoulder. "Stop calling him 'that stupid Swede'! He's not stupid, and there's nothing wrong with coming from Sweden."

Jack stuck his chin out. "Well, you Swedes aren't very good baseballers!"

"You take that back!" Eric yelled.

Walter put one hand on Eric's chest and one on Jack's. "Stop it, you two! We're clubmates, remember?"

Eric stepped back but still glared at Jack. Jack stepped back, too.

Walter looked around at the rest of the Blues. "Is winning the only thing that matters? Don't any of you care about having fun and being friends? Anton might not be the best baseballer, but he helped me get this club together. His father gave us the best bats and balls in town."

No one but Jack met his gaze. Everyone else looked at their shoes or across the road or at the sky.

A couple players began to leave. A couple more followed. Soon everyone was leaving, mumbling and grumbling among themselves.

Walter gave a sigh of relief. At least they weren't going to fight and argue about it anymore—not today, anyway. He glanced over to the other side of the lot, where Polly and the kids had been sitting. They were picking their things up.

Sherman stopped beside him for a minute. Walter was glad Sherman hadn't joined the others in saying nasty things about

Anton. If Sherman had said anything against Anton, all the rest of the boys would have followed Sherman's lead. Besides, he liked Sherman and wanted to stay friends with him.

He smiled at Sherman.

Sherman said quietly, "You really should put someone else on third, you know."

Walter stared after him as he walked across the empty lot through the short weeds to where Jack was waiting for him. Disappointment welled up inside him.

It used to be that playing baseball was a place to get away from the bad things in life for a little while and have fun with his friends. What was happening?

He remembered his friend Lars, Brita's cousin, who had moved back to his family's farm. And Grant, who had moved north. The three of them had loved practicing baseball together.

"I wish they were here now," Walter muttered. "The Blues would be a lot more fun with Lars and Grant on the club. Why does life have to change all the time? When everything is good, why can't life stay that way?"

"That old Jack Griggs was so horrible!" Polly told Brita later in Brita's kitchen. She'd rushed over to Brita's as soon as she got home from the baseball match. She'd already told Brita the whole story about Jack and the other club members wanting to have Anton moved from third base, but she was still mad.

"It sounds like he was awful." Brita folded the shirt she'd just finished ironing and laid it on the clean kitchen work-table. She took another shirt from the wicker basket beside her and laid it on the wooden ironing board. The shirt had been starched and was very stiff and wrinkled. "I'm glad Walter stuck up for him."

"Of course he stuck up for him! They're friends, aren't they?"

"Sometimes it's not so easy to stand up for your friends in front of other people."

Polly stared at her. "You'd stand up for me, wouldn't you?"

"Of course!"

"Well, I'd stand up for you, too."

Brita scowled at her iron. She licked the end of her index finger, then touched her finger to the bottom of the iron quickly. She heaved a sigh that Polly thought sounded like it came all the way from her toes. "The iron is cold already."

Brita set the iron back on the stove top to heat. She slid the wooden handle off, then slid it onto another iron that had been warming on the stove.

"Is your mother working today, too?" Polly asked.

"Yes. She works every day but Sunday, just like most people."

"Does she like her job?"

"She likes sewing, but she has to work very hard. She has to make a certain number of shirts every day. Of course, everybody who works there has a sewing machine, so they can sew very fast."

Polly watched a bead of sweat run from Brita's blond hairline down the side of her face. Ironing was such hot work. She stood by the cast-iron sink while she talked to Brita. She didn't want to be too close to the hot stove on such a warm day.

"Last night," Brita said, "I helped Mama sew buttons on some of the shirts she brought home from work to finish." She looked up from the shirt she was ironing and smiled. "I would rather have been helping you with the Blues' baseball shields."

"Oh! I was so mad at that old Jack Griggs that I forgot to tell you about the baseball shields."

Brita's face lit up with pleasure when she heard how much

Walter and the rest of the Blues liked the shields.

"The captain of the North Stars said he wished his club had shields," Polly added. "Maybe your idea will spread, and all the boys' baseball clubs will have shields one day."

Brita laughed. "Wouldn't that be funny?"

"Even Sherman O'Reily liked them."

"Did he tell you so, right to your face?"

Polly nodded and hoped her face didn't tell how much she liked him. "Yes. He said they were great."

Brita's blue eyes sparkled.

Polly sniffed. "It smells like something is too hot."

"Oh, no!" They both exclaimed at the same time.

Brita grabbed up the iron and groaned. "I scorched the shirt. I guess I forgot to keep the iron moving when we were talking."

"It's only the back of the shirt, and the shirt is dark blue. Maybe it won't be noticed."

"I hope not. Too late now to fix it."

Neither of the girls talked while Brita finished the shirt. While she was folding it, Brita said, "Papa is coming home tomorrow."

"That's wonderful!"

"Since tomorrow is Sunday, Mama will be home all day to help Papa. Dr. Dan is coming over in the afternoon to show Mama how to change Papa's bandages."

"Are you going to learn how to do that, too?"

Brita shook her head. "Papa said he doesn't want Per and me to see him until the bandages come off." She bit her lip and stared at folded, crisp shirts on the tabletop. "Dr. Dan says Papa won't ever look the same as he used to."

Polly couldn't think of anything to say.

"But that's all right." Brita's voice was so quiet that Polly leaned forward to hear her better. "I don't care if Papa doesn't look the same. I only want the burns to stop hurting him."

"Did Dr. Dan say when your father can go back to work?"

"Not for a long time. But even if he can't work, he has to do exercises every day to move the muscles where he was burned. Dr. Dan says that the new skin grows back very tight. If Papa doesn't exercise every day, the skin will be so tight that the muscles won't be able to move anymore."

Polly put a hand on Brita's arm. "Dr. Dan and your father won't let that happen."

Brita smiled at her. Polly saw there were tears in her eyes in spite of the smile. They made her own eyes hot, like she was going to cry, too.

"There's something else."

"What?" A sense of something almost like fear wound its way through Polly's chest and stomach.

"Last night at the hospital after we all visited with Papa, Per and I waited in the hallway while Mama talked with Papa alone. They didn't know we could hear them."

When she paused, Polly asked, "What did they say?"

Brita cleared her throat. Her fingers played with the collar of one of the shirts in the pile on the table. "The money Mama and Per are making isn't enough. If things don't get better soon, I might have to leave school and go to work with Mama as a seamstress."

CHAPTER 10
Walter's Choice

Polly gasped. "But. . .but you can't leave school. You just can't!"

"I don't want to, but if Mama and Papa say I have to, what else can I do?"

Polly stared at her. "It would be awful if we didn't go to school together every day."

"I've always wanted to be a teacher. I won't ever be able to be a teacher if I have to quit school."

"Did you tell your mama and papa that?"

Brita shook her head, biting her bottom lip.

"Maybe you should."

"No. It would sound too selfish. Papa doesn't want to be

out of work, and Mama doesn't want to be a seamstress, and Per doesn't like his work. I'm not going to tell them I can't have a job I don't want, either."

Polly watched silently while Brita pulled a pair of trousers from the wicker basket to iron and chose another hot iron from the stove top.

"I think you're braver than I am," Polly said when Brita had started ironing again.

"I'm not brave. I'm only doing what I have to do. You would do the same thing."

Polly was glad Brita thought she was like that, but she didn't know if Brita was right.

Lying on her bed that night, she stared out at the stars and thought about it. If Brita went to work, they would hardly ever see each other. They didn't have much time together now, since Brita had to help around the house so much. If Brita went to work, they wouldn't even be able to walk to school together. Life would be so lonely without her.

I'm so selfish, she thought, *but I want Brita and me to stay friends.*

The only thing she could do about it was pray. She'd been praying for Brita and her family ever since the fire, and things kept getting worse for them. Still, she didn't know what else to do.

Folding her hands, Polly closed her eyes. "Please, Father God, make the money stretch at Brita's house so she doesn't have to quit school and take a job. Amen."

She rested her arms on the windowsill beside her bed. The stars twinkled down out of a clear sky.

"God," she whispered, "why do some things have to hurt your heart so bad?"

A month passed. School was out for the summer. Chores took

over many of the hours Walter and Polly had spent in school during the fall, winter, and spring.

Sitting on a stump in the Fisk's backyard one day, Polly watched while Walter painted the picket fence that surrounded their yard. Through the open spaces between the pickets, Polly could see into Brita's backyard. She saw Brita come out on her back steps and dump a pail of dirty water over the bush by the back door.

Polly jumped up on top of the stump she'd been sitting on and waved. "Hello, Brita!"

"Hello!" Brita waved back.

"Can you come visit with us for a few minutes?"

"Maybe later. I'm washing the kitchen floor." Brita waved again and went inside.

Disappointed, Polly sat back down on the stump.

"I guess Brita hasn't had to go to work at the seamstress shop with her mother, anyway," Walter said.

"Not yet. Her parents decided it was a good thing to have someone home with her father until he's healed better. Brita can help him do things he can't do for himself yet. And she does most of the household chores, too. They still say she might need to go to work soon, though."

"That's tough."

"How are things at Anton's house?" Polly asked.

"Things are tough there, too." Walter finished spreading white paint over one picket and started on another. "They sold their nice home. Now they live in three small rooms over a grocery store."

"Doesn't his father have a job, either?"

"He's working for another sawmill."

Polly scrunched her eyebrows together. "Then why did they have to move to a smaller house?"

"Because his father used all the money from the sale of

their big house to pay bills the sawmill owed and to pay his employees the money he owed them for working the days before the mill burned."

"Oh."

"He sold the land the sawmill was built on to get more money for the bills. He couldn't rebuild there now even if he had the money."

Polly watched while he finished another picket. "Sometimes, do you feel guilty because things are so bad for all our friends and not for us?"

Walter nodded. "Sometimes, but I wouldn't want those bad things to happen to our family."

"No, I guess I wouldn't, either."

"Hello!"

They both turned in surprise at Sherman's voice. He walked into the yard with a cheerful smile on his freckled face.

"I had to paint our fence last week," he said. "I had about as much paint on the ground as you do."

Walter looked down at the once-green grass and laughed.

"Good thing we're better baseballers than we are painters," Sherman said.

"The Blues have been winning a lot of their games," Polly said.

"It's helped that you and everyone else have been cheering for us," Sherman told her. "It was great that you got some of the other Blues' brothers and sisters to come watch us play."

Walter was surprised at the blush that covered Polly's cheeks. "Polly's always good at talking people into doing things. Like the flag she had us do for the centennial parade two years ago."

"Was that your idea?" Sherman asked Polly.

Polly nodded.

"I remember seeing that. It was terrific."

Polly grinned.

Sherman stuffed his hands into his pockets and shifted his feet about a bit. "Uh, Polly, do you think Brita is ever going to come to another one of our matches?"

"I don't know. She doesn't have much free time anymore. She has to help a lot at home."

"Well, would you ask her if she could come with you to the match Thursday night?" Sherman asked.

"Sure. I'll ask her right now."

Walter watched Polly dart through the back gate, into the alley, through Brita's backyard, and into Brita's house. He turned to Sherman and grinned. "They have no idea of the surprises we have planned for them. Do you have them ready?"

Sherman grinned back. "Yep. My little sister helped me with them."

"Great!"

Sherman's grin died. "Uh, there's something we need to talk about."

Sherman's voice sounded strange. It made Walter's stomach tighten a little. "What?"

"About the Blues, and. . .and Anton."

Walter stared at him. His brush dripped white paint onto the ground, but Walter didn't care. "What about the Blues and Anton?"

Sherman took a deep breath. "Some of the players are saying that if you don't tell Anton to leave the club, they're going to quit."

"Let them quit, then!" Walter stuck the brush in the can, wiped it quickly against the edge, and slapped paint on another picket.

"Walter, some of our best players are talking about leaving."

Walter kept painting. "Who?"

"All the best players except you."

The air seemed to leave Walter's lungs in a rush. His brush stopped at the pointed top of one of the pickets. He stared at the paint dripping down the wood from the bristles. "You, too, Sherman?"

Silence.

Walter turned around slowly and looked into Sherman's face. "You, too?"

Sherman bit his bottom lip and nodded.

Walter sat down hard on the stump Polly had been using. "Why? We've been winning a lot of matches."

"We could win more without Anton. He's the worst player on the club. We lose lots of points to other clubs because of him."

"Do we have to win all our matches? Is that more important than having fun? Is it more important than friendship?"

Sherman ran a hand through his wavy red hair. "I know he's your best friend, but you have to think about the club. Is it fair to ruin everyone else's chances to be on the best club in Minneapolis just to keep from hurting one person's feelings?"

Walter hadn't thought of it that way.

He heard Brita's back door slam and glanced through the slats of the fence. "Polly's coming back," he told Sherman.

She pushed open the back gate and started toward them. Before the gate could slam shut, a little brown-and-white dog slipped into the yard. He dashed after Polly, leaping at her skirt.

Sherman started chuckling. So did Walter. He could tell Polly didn't know Thunder was there.

"Oh!"

Polly almost tumbled backward as Thunder grabbed the end of her long sash in his teeth, pulling out the big bow Polly had tied at the back of her waist.

Walter's chuckle turned into a deep laugh. So did Sherman's.

Thunder tugged at the sash. Polly tugged back. "Let go you. . .you mutt!"

Thunder growled, stuck his rump up in the air, shook his head back and forth, and hung on.

"Don't sit there laughing, Walter. Come help me!"

Walter stumbled over, still laughing. He picked the dog up and stuck him under his arm. "Guess Polly doesn't like you, Thunder."

Polly's mouth dropped. "There really is a Thunder!"

"Told you so."

She examined the end of the sash. "Yuck! He got it all wet." She wrinkled her nose. "Guess I should be glad he didn't tear it."

Walter opened the back gate and put Thunder in the alley.

When Sherman could quit laughing, he asked, "What did Brita say?"

"She'll ask her parents to let her come to the match."

Sherman gave her a big smile. "Great. Tell her to try real hard to get them to let her come."

Polly's head bobbed. "She'll try hard."

"You're coming, too, aren't you?" he asked.

"Of course!"

Sherman took a couple steps backward. "Well, I guess I'll be going. You'll think about what I said, Walter?"

Walter nodded.

"What are you supposed to think about?" Polly asked as Sherman went through the back gate.

Walter shrugged and stood up to start painting again. "Nothing important."

She'll never understand, Walter thought. *She'll say to let Anton stay on the club and let everyone else leave.*

That's what he wanted to do. At least, most of him wanted to do that. But part of him wondered whether Sherman was right. Was it fair to the others to keep Anton on the club? He didn't want to watch the club he'd worked so hard to start fall apart all because of Anton. But he didn't know if he could face telling Anton he couldn't be part of the Blues anymore. His chest hurt thinking of the pain he'd see in Anton's eyes when he told him.

What am I going to do? he thought. *Who do I choose?*

Chapter 11
The Surprise

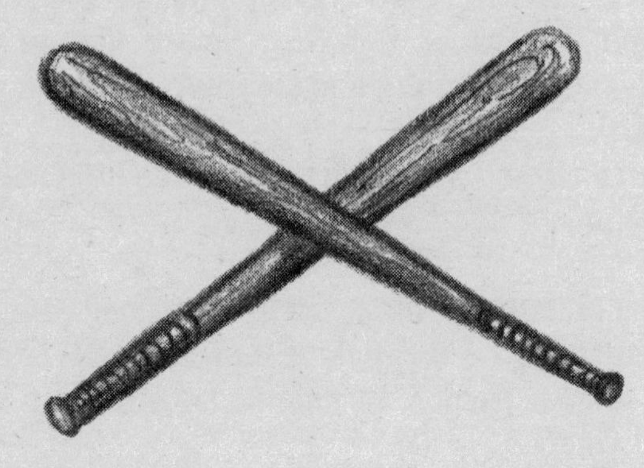

Thursday night, Polly sat down on the blanket beside Brita to wait for the match to begin. She spread her skirt over her legs with the white cotton stockings that came up over her knees.

"I'm so glad my parents let me come tonight!" Brita said, spreading her own skirt modestly over her legs.

"Me, too. It hasn't been nearly as much fun at the matches without you."

Abe and Judith were playing tag all over the lot. They'd gotten to know a lot of the other players' brothers and sisters and didn't pester Polly nearly as much as they did when they first came to the matches with her.

It was an exciting match to watch. The score stayed close from the first inning to the last, but the Blues finally won by one point.

Polly was sorry to see Anton strike out every time he was up to bat. "He seems to get worse every match," she told Brita. "Sometimes I think every time he makes a mistake, it makes him think he won't be able to do it right the next time. So he just makes one mistake after another."

The girls were surprised after the match to see every boy on the Blues club come over to the blanket and form a circle around them. Polly looked at Brita, and Brita looked at Polly. They both started giggling and stood up. "What's going on?" Polly asked.

Sherman cleared his throat. "We wanted to thank you both for making our shields. So we pooled our money and bought you these."

Sherman handed Polly a package wrapped in brown paper and tied with twine. Walter handed a package just like it to Brita.

Polly's hands trembled from excitement when she tried to untie the twine.

"We would have given them to you sooner," Sherman said, "but it took us awhile to get together enough money."

"You didn't need to give us anything," Polly said.

"No." Brita was struggling with the knot in the twine binding her own package. "We wanted to make the shields for you. It was fun. But Polly made most of them."

"It was Brita's idea, though," Polly reminded them.

Polly and Brita finally undid the knots. They unwrapped the gifts at the same time.

"An autograph book!" Polly exclaimed.

"I've wanted one for the longest time." Brita ran a hand over the soft cover of her book.

"Me, too," Polly said. "Simply *all* the girls have them."

The boys grinned at the girls and each other.

"Open them up," Anton said.

They did. On the first page of each book was a rhyme and the signature of every boy on the club.

Polly glanced at Brita's page and smiled. "You wrote the same thing in each book." She read the rhyme aloud:

"Remember us is all we ask,
But should remembrance prove a task,
Forget us."

Polly laughed. "We won't forget you."

The boys grinned and started wandering off toward their homes.

While Polly was shaking out the blanket, she overheard Sherman talking to Walter. "The guys decided not to say anything today because it was a special day for the girls and all. But they want an answer from you soon."

"What was that all about?" Polly asked when Sherman left.

"Nothing," Walter answered.

"Then why does your face look like a thundercloud?"

Walter shrugged and started untying his shield. "I guess I have a lot on my mind."

Puzzled, Polly stared at him as he and Anton gathered up the bats. They never kept secrets from each other, except for surprises like the one the boys had for her and Brita today. From the dark look in Walter's eyes, she didn't think this was that kind of secret.

Something was wrong, but what?

Polly was finishing up the supper dishes the next evening when Brita rushed through the back door and into the kitchen in tears.

"What's wrong?" Polly asked, wiping her hands on the linen dish towel.

"My. . .my. . .my. . .," Brita stuttered through the sobs that shook her body from head to toe.

"Did your parents decide you have to go to work with your mother at the seamstress shop?"

Brita shook her head.

Polly was glad her parents and Abe and Dr. Dan and his family were all in the family living room. She knew Brita would have been embarrassed to have them see her crying.

She put her arm around Brita's shoulders and led her to a chair. "Sit down." She handed her the dish towel. "You can use this to wipe your face."

It was a couple minutes before Brita stopped sobbing long enough to talk.

"It. . ." Sob. Sniff. "It. . .it's my papa."

Polly frowned. "At supper tonight, Dr. Dan said he took your father's bandages off this afternoon. He didn't say there was anything wrong."

"It's his face." Sniff. "It's horribly scarred."

Polly swallowed the lump that suddenly appeared in her throat. "I thought you knew it was going to be scarred."

Brita nodded. "But I didn't know it would be this bad. It's so terrible I can hardly stand to look at him."

Polly patted her hand and tried to think of something to say.

"Dr. Dan said Papa's skin will look better when it's healed more, but he says the skin will never look normal again."

"I'm sorry," Polly murmured, wishing desperately that she could say or do something to make Brita stop hurting.

"I didn't think it would matter to me what his face looked like," Brita said. "But I can't look at him without staring and wanting to cry."

"I'd feel the same way if it were my father," Polly told her.

"I'm sure anyone would."

"I feel like such a terrible person. I. . .I'm almost afraid of him. I don't want to even touch him."

Polly blinked back tears.

"Polly, do you think. . .do you think I don't love my papa anymore?"

Polly tried to speak but couldn't right away. Her throat ached from the tears she was trying not to cry for her friend. "I know you love him, Brita."

"Then why do I feel these terrible things?"

"I guess because you didn't know how bad his face was going to look. You'll get used to it after awhile, and then you won't be afraid of him anymore."

"Do you truly believe that?"

"Of course."

"Polly, could you love somebody who looked. . .scary?"

"I think I could if I knew the person wasn't scary inside," Polly answered slowly. "Before the fire, you didn't love your papa because of the way he looked, did you?"

Brita shook her head. "I loved him because he was Papa, and he loved me."

"That hasn't changed."

Brita shook her head again, but Polly didn't think she looked like she was sure.

"Keep remembering how much he loves you," Polly told her, squeezing her friend's hand.

Brita squeezed it back and hung on tight. They sat that way together for a long time, not saying anything.

Dear Father God, Polly prayed silently, *please help Brita, and show me how to help her, too. Amen.*

Chapter 12
The Great Wheel

"It was awful, Walter," Polly told him the next afternoon as they walked to the lot where the Blues were meeting. "Brita felt so guilty that she's afraid of her father."

"She should feel guilty."

"Walter!"

"Well, he's her father. What does it matter what he looks like?" What Polly had told him about Brita made Walter so mad that he could feel his chest filling up with anger.

"I know you're right, but she can't help how she feels, can she?"

"Her father can't help it he's scarred, either. Brita should be glad he's alive. Eighteen men died in that explosion and fire. Would she rather he was dead like them?"

"Of course not! What an awful thing to say!"

Walter snorted. "I think it's awful of Brita to feel like she does about her father. She should try using Anton's father's question."

"What question?"

"When Anton's father doesn't know what to do about something, he asks himself, 'What would Jesus do?' "

"That's a good question to ask," Polly admitted, "but I think Brita knows what Jesus would do. Jesus would love her father no matter how he looked."

"Then shouldn't Brita?"

"She knows she should. She wants to. She's just having trouble doing it."

Walter didn't understand that at all. He'd always thought Brita was nice. He'd never have thought she'd act so awful about her father.

I wish Polly hadn't come along tonight, Walter thought as they reached the lot. At least Abe and Judith weren't along for a change. Usually he liked Polly's company. Today, however, he knew the guys would demand a decision about Anton. He didn't want her around when they did.

He'd thought and thought about Anton and about what Sherman had said. *Sherman is right,* he thought. *I can't let everyone on the club down for one person.*

But his decision didn't make him happy. It made him mad that he was forced to choose between the club he loved and his best friend. The anger kept rolling around inside him like boiling water in a kettle.

"Hi, Walter! Hi, Polly!"

Walter's glance darted to Anton, who was jogging across the dirt street toward them with a friendly smile.

Walter's stomach tightened. "I thought you told me you couldn't practice with us today."

"I did." Anton started walking beside Walter. "The man who owns the grocery store beneath where we live asked *For* to paint the storm windows for him. Um, *For* does odd jobs for people now, in the evenings when he's done with his job at the sawmill. We. . .we need the extra money."

Walter frowned. "I thought *you* were painting the windows."

"I am. *For* doesn't get off work until six o'clock, and sometimes later, so he told me I should start on them."

"So, why aren't you painting the storm windows?"

Anton grinned. "The grocer's wife decided she wants a different color paint than the grocer chose, so we have to wait for her to buy it."

Polly laughed.

Anton's grin faded. "At first, I wasn't going to come, even when the grocer told me I didn't need to paint this afternoon. But the Blues and baseball are the best things in my life right now."

Polly and Anton chatted while the three of them walked. Walter didn't pay any attention to what they were saying. He was too busy feeling bad and wishing both Polly and Anton would go home so he wouldn't have to feel so guilty.

They passed from blocks filled with two-story wooden houses to a block filled with businesses. Horse-drawn wagons, some with tops and some without, rumbled by on their wooden wheels. Horses attached to driverless wagons stood patiently beside the stoops where they were tied in front of the business houses. Their tails swished to brush away the ever-present flies.

One such horse, in front of a saddle and harness shop, whinnied and stuck his large, bay-colored head toward Walter. "Hello, boy. Getting lonely waiting for your master?" he asked, brushing its nose.

He liked the strong smell of the horse and the smell of

leather from the horse's harness. *A guy should have a dog or a horse to talk to when he can't talk to anyone else,* Walter thought. He ran a hand along the back of the horse's head and had the strangest feeling that he wanted to bury his face in its neck and cry.

Instead he gave the horse an extra pat and started walking again. Polly and Anton were a step or two in front of him now, but Walter didn't try to catch up to them. He let his fingers run lightly along the sides of the barrels that lined the wooden sidewalk in front of most of the stores and tried not to think about what was ahead.

The closer they got to the lot, the slower Walter walked. But when they were half a block away, boys' shouts and laughter drew his curious gaze.

A bicycle with a front wheel taller than Walter dashed out from the empty lot onto the wooden sidewalk. Sherman was astride it, his red hair gleaming in the sunshine.

"A great wheel!" Walter exclaimed.

"I'd love to have one of those," Anton said.

Polly laughed. "Look at the funny little back wheel. It looks like a tiny tail on the end of a big dog."

"A curly tail," Anton added.

"Why is the front wheel so big?" she asked.

"The bigger the front wheel, the faster the bicycle can go," Anton explained.

"Catch it!" Sherman called out. He swung one leg over the top of the huge front wheel and dropped to the ground.

Polly gasped. "Why did he do that?"

"Great wheels don't have brakes," Walter told her.

Jack and Eric grabbed at the great wheel but couldn't keep it from falling. Sherman didn't seem to mind. With the help of Jack and Eric, he picked it up again. He wheeled it up beside a building and leaned it against the wall. "Who wants to try it next?"

"I do!" Walter called out, along with several other boys.

Walter could hardly believe it when Sherman grinned at him and said, "You first."

While the great wheel leaned against the wall, Walter climbed up. His heart leaped to his throat when he looked down and saw how far he was above the ground. But it was a good kind of excitement he felt, not fear.

"Don't lean on the handlebars," Sherman warned. "That will throw you off balance. Unless you're going up a hill. Then you should lean forward."

"How can you keep from leaning forward if you go down a hill?" Walter asked.

Sherman pointed toward the top of the wheel. "See those things sticking out on both sides?"

Walter nodded.

"Those are footrests. When you go down a hill, you put your feet on them and lean far back. If you lean forward going down a hill, you're apt to wind up going down the hill on your nose."

A minute later, Walter was wobbling over the bumpy lot, high above the other boys. His heart raced faster than his feet when he ran around the bases.

He didn't dare ride in the street with the horses and wagons that passed. He tried to head the bike toward the sidewalk, thinking that would be smoother to ride on, but it wasn't easy to get where he wanted to go.

He bit his bottom lip, trying to concentrate on everything at once. Was anything in his path, like a rock or rut, that would make the wheel turn and throw him off?

"Get out of the way!" he yelled to the boys who were running along beside him and darting back and forth in front of him.

"Oops!" Walter almost forgot not to lean forward on the handlebars.

The great wheel bounced up onto the sidewalk beside the wagon store. "Finally!" He breathed a sigh of relief as the bike clattered over the wood.

"Oh, no!"

A woman was coming down the walk pushing a baby buggy! Walter glanced around frantically for something to stop him. He grabbed at one of the wooden posts that held up the wooden awning in front of the shop. It only slowed him down a bit and set the front wheel to weaving back and forth.

Keeping one hand on the handlebars, Walter leaned out farther to grab the next post. Caught it! The front wheel tipped against a wooden barrel.

Walter took a deep shaky breath and looked at where he'd last seen the woman and baby carriage. They were still there. The woman's hands clutched the carriage handle. Her mouth was hanging open. Her eyes were huge as she stared at him.

He smiled at her.

She started pushing her carriage again. She stared at him and the great wheel as she walked slowly past.

"That was a great job," Sherman said, running up to him. "Quick thinking, stopping it that way."

Sherman held the bicycle while Walter climbed down on top of the barrel, then jumped to the ground.

All the boys on the club had a chance to try the great wheel—that is, all of them who dared. Most of them weren't as fortunate as Walter had been in stopping it and fell or jumped off instead.

"I wish I could try riding it," Polly told Walter. "But Sherman said my skirt would get caught in the spokes."

Anton was the last to try it. Walter thought Anton rode it better than anyone except Sherman. Anton's face shined with excitement while he rode.

Anton's smile made Walter feel terrible. Sherman, Jack, and

the others who threatened to leave the club were acting like Anton was their friend, like any of the other club members. All the while, they were planning to throw Anton off the club.

Riding the great wheel put the whole Blues club in a good mood. They were excited when they started the match against the Mississippis, the same club they'd played the first match of the year. This time, they won.

Dread filled Walter's chest like a big ball when he saw Sherman and Jack walking toward him after the match. The rest of the boys and Polly were gathered around Sherman's great wheel.

Sherman stuck his hands in the pockets of his knickerbockers. "Time to tell us your decision, Walter."

Jack swaggered up beside him and grinned. "Guess we already know what that will be. When are you goin' to tell the Swede we don't need any lousy baseballers who aren't born Americans on our club?"

Walter's hands clenched into fists at his sides.

Sherman stuck a palm out toward Jack and frowned.

I guess Sherman doesn't like the way it sounds when Jack puts it into words, Walter thought, *but Sherman feels the same way.* "I haven't decided when to tell him."

Sherman put a hand on his shoulder. "Well, you can tell him whenever you want, but maybe you should tell him before the next match if you don't want the other guys to hurt his feelings."

What would Jesus do?

The words shot through Walter's mind. Guilt shot through his chest. He thought he knew what Jesus would do.

"See you later," Sherman said, walking away.

"Yeah, see ya." Jack gave him that superior grin of his that made Walter want to slug him.

Walter stared after them, clenching his fists. If he did what he thought Jesus would do, the Blues would lose their best players. Sherman, the most popular kid in school, might not be his friend anymore. And Sherman's other friends might not be his friends anymore, either.

Anton was standing by the great wheel beside Eric, laughing and looking happier than Walter had seen him in a long time. He'd even played better today than he had all summer.

Lose Anton's friendship or the friendship of Sherman and all Sherman's friends. What a lousy choice! Walter thought his chest would explode it hurt so bad.

What would Jesus do? He wished the words would stop running through his mind.

Was this what it was like for Brita? He'd told Polly that he thought Brita was terrible for not doing what she thought Jesus would do. He'd thought she was disloyal to her father. Now he was being disloyal to his best friend.

He took a deep, shaky breath. "Sherman, wait up!"

Sherman and Jack turned around. Walter jogged over to them. He stopped about two feet away. Ignoring Jack, he looked straight into Sherman's green Irish eyes. "Anton's staying with the Blues."

"What?" Jack brushed at the dirty hair that fell over his forehead. "You'd choose that stupid Swede over us?"

Walter stuck out his chin. "Any day."

"You know what this means," Sherman said quietly. "We weren't kidding about leaving the Blues."

"I know."

Sherman shrugged, turned around, and walked toward his great wheel.

Jack spat at the ground in front of Walter's dust-covered shoes. "You'll be sorry. This club will never win another match."

Probably not, Walter thought, watching Jack follow Sherman. The thought made him sad.

The other players who had threatened to leave looked at

Sherman expectantly. He shrugged again. "Guess we're done with the Blues, boys."

"What!"

"What's going on?"

"Done? What do ya mean?"

The other players stared at him, puzzled.

"Walter will tell you all about it," Jack said with that nasty smile.

Sherman took off his Blues shield and handed it to Polly, who looked stunned. He climbed up on his great wheel.

"Good luck without us, Swede lovers! You'll need all the luck you can get!" Jack ran alongside Sherman's great wheel, not bothering to give back his shield.

The others handed Polly their shields or dropped them on the ground beside her. Some gave Walter dirty looks and made nasty comments as they left.

Polly looked at Walter. He saw the hurt, bewildered look in her eyes and looked away. Why did doing what he thought Jesus wanted him to do have to hurt people he liked?

When the others had left, Anton, Erik, and the few remaining players stared at Walter, waiting for him to tell them what had happened.

I can't tell them that the others left because of Anton, Walter thought. *That would embarrass Anton and hurt him just as much as if I'd told him to leave the club.*

He stuffed his hands in his trouser pockets and cleared his throat. "They decided they don't want to play with us anymore."

"Why not?" Anton asked.

Walter shrugged. "They want to play with kids who are better baseball players than we are." *At least that's part of the truth.*

The happy looks that had filled everyone's faces after playing with the great wheel and winning the match were gone now.

"That stinks," one of the players said.

"Yah, now we don't have enough good players left to win anymore," someone else said.

"It's because so many of us are Swedish, isn't it?" Erik asked, his eyes flashing.

"We can still have fun playing," Walter said. He didn't want to answer Erik's question directly.

"That's right," Erik agreed. "I say good riddance to them. If they don't want us, we don't want them."

No one else spoke up to agree with him. Everyone but Anton and Polly just picked up their things and left quietly.

Walter's eyes grew hot. He blinked back tears, unwilling to let anyone see him cry. He'd done what he believed was right. *Still, it's like watching the club I've worked for so hard die,* Walter thought. *Why does life have to be so hard sometimes, God?*

Chapter 13
The Monster Man

Polly was glad the next day was Sunday. Sitting in the church with the sun streaming through the tall stained glass windows and singing the hymns with the rest of the congregation felt good.

"It reminds me of the good people and good things there are in the world, even when things are bad," she'd told Walter one day. "Mostly, it reminds me that God loves us, even when it doesn't feel like He does."

This morning is one of those times it doesn't feel like God loves us, she thought, looking across the aisle at Brita's family. They were seated three rows closer to the front than Polly's family, so it was easy to see them. Polly saw a lot of other people watching them, too. Rather, they were staring at Mr. Swenson.

"Look, Mommy," the little girl with long brown braids seated in front of Polly had said, pointing to Mr. Swenson when the Swensons took their seat. "Is that man the monster man from the circus?"

The mother's face beneath her Sunday hat had turned beet red. "No. Shhhh!"

But Polly noticed the little girl had continued to stare at Mr. Swenson, and so had the mother and father.

Polly was ashamed to find it was hard for her not to stare, too. Mr. Swenson's face did look very bad with all the scars. He didn't have the beard and mustache he'd always had before the fire. They would have helped hide the scarring. Polly made herself watch the pastor instead of Mr. Swenson.

When the service was over, people still stared at Mr. Swenson as he walked down the aisle. The little girl with the brown braids stood at the end of her pew and looked right up at him. "You look scary."

"Sorry," Mr. Swenson said in a low voice.

Brita glared at the girl and grabbed her father's hand.

The little girl's mother took her hand and scolded her, but it was too late to stop her words from hurting Brita and her family. Polly thought her heart would break for them.

"If it were only kids treating Papa that way, maybe it wouldn't be so bad," Brita told Polly a few minutes later while they stood outside waiting for their parents.

Polly bounced Dr. Dan's son, Richard, up and down on her hip. She was glad to see her parents, Walter's parents, and Dr. Dan and his pretty wife, Marcia, were visiting with Mr. Swenson as if everything was normal. Of course, they'd all been to see him at his home, so his looks weren't a surprise to them anymore.

"This is your father's first time out in public since he was burned," Polly reminded Brita. "People will get used to him after awhile and not stare."

"I don't know," Brita said slowly. "I'm not used to the way he looks yet."

Richard squirmed about in Polly's arms, trying to see everyone and everything at once. "Oof. He's heavy."

Brita held out her arms toward him. "I'll hold him for a while."

Polly was glad to let her friend hold Richard. After the heavy little boy was in Brita's arms, Polly shook her own arm. "My arm was almost asleep. I like watching him, but he's growing so fast and getting so plump and heavy."

Brita bounced Richard up and down. He giggled at her and threw his arms about her neck. Brita looked over his tiny shoulder at Polly. "My parents told me last night that I have to go to work with Mama. Mama already talked to her boss, and he said he would hire me."

"Oh, Brita, I'm so sorry!" Polly was sorry for her and sorry for herself, too. "When are we going to see each other?"

"Maybe you can come talk to me when I do chores around the house. Papa said he won't let me work as many hours as Mama, even though there are girls our age who sew there for ten and twelve hours every day."

"That's good of your father, but I wish you didn't have to work there at all."

"Papa says maybe, when he gets a job again, I can quit working there and go back to school. We'll have to see."

Brita didn't look as unhappy about it as Polly thought she would. "It would be worse if I was starting the job during school and had to quit seeing everyone right away."

Polly thought it was bad enough now.

A few minutes later when Brita and Polly joined the adults, Richard stared at Brita's father's face just as everyone else had done. Polly saw Brita's lips, which had been smiling at Richard only a minute earlier, turn down at the corners.

Richard reached his fat little arms toward Mr. Swenson. Mr. Swenson took him in his good arm and settled the youngster against his hip.

Brita shared a surprised look with Polly.

Richard lifted a chubby hand and laid it very, very gently against Mr. Swenson's cheek. "Owie. Owie hurt?"

"No, little Richard, it doesn't hurt too much."

Mr. Swenson smiled at Richard with the side of his face that wasn't burned. The other side stayed stiff.

Polly thought she saw tears glisten in one of his eyes, but only for a moment. She wasn't sure. They might have been the tears she was blinking out of her own eyes.

That evening, when dinner and dishes were behind them and the long summer daylight was almost gone, Brita's and Polly's families sat out on Polly's wide front porch and visited in the twilight. Insects chirped a song for them. Fireflies could just begin to be seen flashing their yellow lights.

"Can Brita and I go for a walk?" Polly asked.

"Yes, as long as you're not gone too long," her mother answered.

Mrs. Swenson agreed.

"I'm glad we can talk alone," Brita said when they'd gone a couple houses down the block. "Sunday evenings are the only time I seem to have time to relax anymore."

She talked quietly. Even though they were alone, there were people sitting on most of the front steps, enjoying the pretty, quiet evening weather. The girls were used to that.

Almost everyone spent time on their front porches together at the end of the warm summer evenings.

"Do you go to work with your mother tomorrow morning?" Polly asked.

"Yes."

"I guess we won't have time to work on that surprise for Walter and the Blues anymore, then."

"Probably not." Brita shrugged. "It was just a joke anyway, wasn't it?"

"I guess."

Polly didn't know what to say after that, so she just kept walking quietly beside Brita.

"Do you remember what Richard did after church today?" Brita asked. "I mean, the way he touched Papa's face?"

"Yes."

"He was the only one who didn't act like Papa is a monster. Even I've acted like he was a monster." Brita gulped. "When I saw Richard touch Papa's face, I remembered that I hadn't even hugged Papa since the bandages came off his face."

"Oh," Polly said in a little voice.

"After church today, I hugged Papa and told him I love him."

Polly gave a sigh of relief. "Good."

"Only. . .only inside me, the way his face looks still bothers me. I wish it didn't. I don't want to feel about him the way those people do who stared at him so rudely today."

"I know that."

"Polly, you're so good. You haven't ever said you have bad feelings like this about your papa because he only has one leg. Did you ever think bad things about him and his leg? Do people ever stare at him like they do at my papa?"

Polly thought for a minute. "It was different with my father. He lost his leg in the War Between the States, before I was born. I've never known him with two legs."

"Oh."

"He has a cork leg, and his trousers cover it, of course, so it's not out in plain sight like your father's face."

"I know."

"He can't walk as good as other people, though. He needs his cane, and he walks kind of jerky, 'cause he can't bend his cork leg. So people can tell there's something wrong. Sometimes they ask him about it. He doesn't mind."

"But I guess they don't tell him he looks scary, like that little girl told Papa at church this morning."

"No, but sometimes they stare at him rudely, like they do your father. Or they push past him when he's walking and knock him off balance. Sometimes people even act like he's not as smart as they are, as though a person kept their brains in their legs instead of their head."

Brita stared at her, her blue eyes wide. "Surely not!"

Polly nodded. "Oh, yes. I remember once when I went with Father to the bank where he works, an old lady in a fine dress and fancy hat came up to me. She asked me—right in front of Father—whether it wasn't awful to have a father with a peg leg!"

Brita's eyes snapped. "I hope you kicked her right in the shins!"

Polly laughed. "I wanted to, but I didn't. When she left, Father smiled about it and said, 'I guess it's better to have a wooden leg than a wooden brain.' "

Brita laughed.

"I think her words still hurt him, even though he joked about it," Polly said. It still made her sad inside to remember it. "I hate when people hurt Father's feelings," she whispered.

Brita squeezed her hand. "I know. I hate when people hurt my papa's feelings, too."

"I asked Father once what it was like to have only one leg."

"What did he say?"

"He said sometimes he missed doing things he could do with two legs, but that wasn't what hurt him most. What hurt most was when people treated him badly. He said he thinks that's what hurts everybody most—whether their body has been hurt or not."

They walked along together without talking for a little way. Polly could hear people talking quietly on their porches, insects buzzing, and dogs barking in the distance. Windows were squares of soft yellow light as people lit their lamps against the night.

"I don't want to hurt Papa," Brita said finally. "But how can I change myself and stop noticing the way he looks?"

Polly thought for a minute. "Maybe you could think about the things you like about him instead."

"But when I look at him, I forget everything but what he looks like and how much the fire hurt him."

"Well, maybe you could make a list of the things you like. You could even write them down to help remember them."

Brita sighed. "I wish God would just take my bad feelings away. I prayed that He would."

"Mother says that sometimes instead of changing things by Himself, God gives us ways to help change things. Like when she was a girl our age. She didn't like slavery. God gave her a chance to help a slave get free. But it didn't just happen. Mother had to help her hide. It was very dangerous."

"Goodness! I guess if your mama could do that, I can try making a list." Brita smiled.

Polly smiled back. "I'm glad God let us meet each other and be friends."

"Me, too."

A warm feeling filled Polly's chest. It was good to have a friend.

CHAPTER 14
The Girls' Secret

Walter picked up a flat, yellow rock from beside the lake and tossed it out over the blue water. *Splish! Splish! Splish!*

"Three skips. Not bad," he murmured. "Too bad I can't pitch a baseball as well as that."

Since Sherman had left the Blues, there wasn't a boy on the club that could pitch worth a penny.

He stared out over the water. Sunlight danced over the lake, making it look like a bed of sparkling diamonds. Green bulrushes stood tall out of the water. He could hear voices and laughter from where his family as well as Polly's, Dr. Dan's, and Brita's families were still sitting around on blankets under the trees where they'd picnicked after church.

"Walter, come back and join us!" Per called to him.

Walter walked back slowly. He wasn't in a mood for family and friends. He wanted to be alone, but he knew if he said so, they'd pester him all the more to join them.

Per was waiting for him on the edge of the group. "So why are you so glum?"

Walter hadn't meant to tell anyone, but he liked and trusted Per. The story about the Blues started tumbling out. Before long, everyone had stopped talking and was listening to Walter.

"We haven't won a match since Sherman and his friends left," Walter said, coming to the end of his story. "All the boys on the club are tired of playing. It isn't any fun anymore."

"Do you have to win every match to have fun?" Walter's father asked.

"No, but it's more fun if you think you have a chance to win *some*times. Sherman and the others started their own club, the Reds. They're already so good that they win most of their matches."

"Do you have a coach?" Per asked.

Walter shook his head.

"Do you think it would help if I coached the Blues?" Per offered. "Of course, I could only do it when I wasn't working."

A sliver of hope lightened Walter's heart. "Would you?"

"Sure."

"I don't know, Son," Per and Brita's father said. He leaned back against a tree trunk, his broad-brimmed hat helping the tree shade his scars from the sun. "If someone in our family is going to coach the Blues, I think it should be me. After all, I'm the best ballplayer in this family." His one-sided grin showed he was teasing.

Still, his statement sent a shock through the group. Walter could feel it. Everyone stared at Mr. Swenson as though he'd lost his senses. He couldn't move his badly scarred arm and hand enough to play ball, and everyone at the picnic but little Richard knew it.

Polly's father cleared his throat. "I don't know about that, Ole. I expect you can hit and catch a ball about as well as I can run around the bases."

How could Uncle Enoch say that? Walter wondered. He couldn't run around bases with a wooden leg! How could he joke about something like that?

Brita's father chuckled.

Walter stared at him in amazement. Did he think it was funny?

"I guess you've called that right, Enoch," Brita's father said around his chuckle.

Walter wondered whether Polly's and Brita's fathers' disabilities made them feel closer to each other. Did they understand each other in a way other people couldn't understand them? Was that why they could say things to each other that would hurt them if other people said them?

"I used to hit a mean baseball in my younger days, though," Brita's father was saying. "I might not be able to hit and catch much anymore, but I can probably see what the players on Walter's club are doing wrong and tell them what they can do to improve."

"We need all the help we can get," Walter told him. "You and Per can both coach the Blues. Wish we could get a few more players, too. The club is pretty small since the others left."

Abe leaped to his feet. "I'll play!"

Walter shook his head. "I told you, you're too young."

"But I'll try real hard."

"You're younger than everyone else on the club," Walter told him. "Smaller, too. Maybe in a year or two."

Abe kicked hard at a dandelion, knocking its yellow top into the air. "Aw, shucks!"

"Abraham Stevenson!" His mother's head jerked toward the curly-haired boy. "Don't let me ever hear you use words like that again!"

Abe shifted his shoulders. "I didn't know that was one of the bad words."

"It's not one of the worst, Son," his father said, "but it's not one of the best, either."

"I could play on the Blues," Polly said. "So could Brita, when she isn't working, that is."

"Me, too!" Judith piped up.

"Oh, sure," Walter said with a grin. "The kids who left the club think Swedish kids can't play baseball. They'd laugh the club off the field if we had girls running around the bases in skirts!"

Per started laughing. Walter joined him, thinking of skirts and braids flying while the girls tried to outrace a ball to base.

Abe saw Per and Walter, and he started laughing, too. He slapped his knee, grabbed his stomach, and bent over from the waist, laughing. Pretty soon, Walter wasn't sure whether he was laughing at Polly's offer or at Abe!

"Why don't we have a match?" Uncle Enoch asked. "Right here and now. The adults against the kids."

"Sounds good to me," Walter's father said. "Walter brought his bat and ball."

Walter nodded. "I was only going to practice hitting a few balls by myself, but I think it will be fun to play."

Per nudged him with his elbow. "Yah. We'll show you old-timers how to do it right."

"Old-timers!" his father said. "Well, I guess we'll show

you young whippersnappers a thing or two."

Per, Walter, Uncle Enoch, and Dr. Dan found some large rocks at the water's edge to be used for bases and set up a diamond in a meadow near the trees where they'd picnicked.

The adults were up to bat first. Walter was chosen pitcher for the kids' side. Per had the always dangerous job of catcher.

Enoch Stevenson, Polly's father, was the first batsman. Polly's mother, Tina, was selected to run in his place.

He took a couple practice swings, then pointed to the area right in front of his waist. "Put it here!" he called to Walter.

Walter threw the ball, but not as hard as usual. He felt almost guilty pitching to his uncle Enoch. After all, he had that wooden leg.

Crack! Uncle Enoch hit the ball squarely. It went flying out into left field where Judith was playing. She missed catching it and had to chase it through the long meadow grass.

Aunt Tina ran toward first base, holding her long skirt up above her ankles, the grass swishing as she hurried through it.

"Keep going, Tina!" Uncle Enoch called as she reached first. Aunt Tina headed on toward second.

Walter watched Judith, bent over, still chasing the ball. Finally she held it up and tried to throw it to the nearest player, Abe, at second. She only managed to throw it a few feet. Abe had to run out to get it.

Walter groaned. *And Polly thinks it would help to let girls play on the Blues!* he thought.

"Keep going, Tina!" Uncle Enoch called again as Aunt Tina reached second. She headed for third.

Abe grabbed the ball and threw it to third. Polly caught it right after her mother touched the rock marking third base. "Too bad!" Aunt Tina said to her daughter with a grin.

Walter settled his hands on his hips and stared at Uncle Enoch. "Good hit!" he called.

Enoch smiled. "When I was in the War Between the States, we played baseball in the camps. I managed to hit a couple balls back then."

I won't hurl such an easy pitch to you next time, Walter told him silently.

Mrs. Swenson was up next. She whiffed the first four pitches, in spite of her husband's coaching, and was out.

Dr. Dan's wife, Marcia, was next. She whiffed the first couple balls but managed to hit the third. It went foul. Two more whiffs, and she was out, too.

Dr. Dan followed his wife to bat. Walter didn't want him to hit the ball, not with Polly's mother on third base. He tried to throw balls and walk him.

The first three pitches were balls, just like he wanted. But it was hard to throw the nine balls needed to walk a batsman. On the fourth throw, Dr. Dan hit the ball out into right field.

Abe raced from second base to help Judith find the ball. Walter ran from the pitcher's mound to second base to cover for Abe. He could hear Dr. Dan running through the grass, heading past Brita at first and toward second.

He knew Aunt Tina was heading home. She ran slow in her high-heeled, high-buttoned shoes. Still, Abe would never be able to throw the ball all the way to the catcher and put his mother out.

Abe grabbed up the ball.

"Throw it here!" Walter yelled.

Abe threw. Walter had to leap two feet to the left to catch it. Two feet that meant Dr. Dan hit second base before Walter could tag him out.

Walter breathed a sigh of relief when he saw that his mother was the next batsman. He was sure she couldn't hit a ball into the outfield!

He was right. After a few whiffs and balls, she did manage

to nick the ball. It rolled a few feet toward him before Per caught it up and tagged her out.

Walter grinned when his father came to bat next. It was going to be hard to try to strike him out, but fun!

"Need a nap first?" he hollered to his father.

"This old-timer is ready any time you are," his father called to him from home base.

"Here's the whippersnapper hurler's best shot!" Walter called back.

Father swung hard. *Whiff!*

The kids cheered wildly.

Crack! Mr. Fisk connected with the next pitch.

Walter saw it coming straight toward him, a couple feet above his head. He barely had time to think before leaping up and catching it with both hands. The third out!

"Great catch!" Per called.

With a light heart, Walter jogged toward home base. The other kids joined him there to take their turn at bat while the adults took to the field. Walter and Per put their heads together to decide the batting line up.

"The girls are sure to be at least as bad at hitting the ball as their mothers," Per said. "Let's go girl, boy, girl, boy. That way, maybe we won't have three outs right in a row."

They selected Judith for first batsman. Just as they suspected, she whiffed the first four balls, even though Uncle Enoch sent her slow pitches.

Abe went next. After a couple balls, a whiff, and a foul ball, he made a solid hit. His mother raced through the meadow grass after the ball while Abe ran to second base, laughing all the way.

Per and Walter exchanged "here we go again" glances when Polly went to bat.

Whack! She hit the first pitch. The ball sailed between first and second but not far into the outfield.

She dropped the bat and ran for first. Judith and Brita's yells cheered her on. She stopped at first, safe and grinning.

Walter and Per looked at each other with lifted eyebrows. "Did you see what I saw?" Walter asked.

"It was a fluke," Per said, shaking his head.

"Had to be," Walter agreed.

He was up next. With Abe on second and Polly on first, he sure hoped he hit a strong ball, long past Dr. Dan in the outfield.

After one whiff and two balls, he did just that. Abe made it home and Polly to third base. Walter was headed toward second when he saw that Dr. Dan had the ball and was throwing it to Aunt Tina at second. He turned and raced back toward first, the long meadow grass whipping at his trousers. He made it safely and stayed put.

Brita was up next.

Oh, well, Walter thought. *It will only be our second out, and Per is up after her.*

Brita whiffed the first pitch, just as he suspected. "Relax, Brita!" he called. "Watch the ball!"

Enoch pitched.

Whack! The ball whizzed past his head, just inside the base.

Walter was so surprised that he forgot to run.

"Move, Walter!"

Per's yell jerked him into action. He headed toward second, swinging his head to see what happened to the ball. Time to try for third! He kept going. Made it!

Polly had made it home, too. Looking back, he saw Brita safe on second. "Good hit, Brita!" he called.

She smiled and waved.

Per was up next. Walter grinned. "I'm as good as home," he told his mother, who was playing third base.

Per hit a couple foul balls, then hit a ball right to Dr. Dan. Dan caught it and tossed it to Walter's father, the catcher.

Walter saw the gleam in his father's eyes when he tagged him out.

The rest of the match went about the same. In the end, the kids won, but by only one run.

Everyone was tired and happy by then. The women's hair was slipping from their buns. The men's shirts were rumpled. No one seemed to care.

"I had more fun playing today than I've had playing with the Blues all summer," Walter told Per.

When everyone was lying in the grass resting, Walter asked Polly, "Where did you and Brita learn to hit a ball like that, anyway?"

Polly and Brita grinned at each other. "Dr. Dan and Brita's father taught us," Polly told him.

The two men smiled. "Surprise!"

Per looked at Walter out of the corner of his eye. "We've been had."

"But good," Walter agreed. He stuck out his hand toward Polly. "Welcome to the Blues, girls."

Polly pushed herself to her knees. "You mean it?"

Walter nodded. It made him feel good to see the happy light in her eyes.

"What about me?" Abe asked, sitting up.

Walter laughed. "You're too young. How many times do I have to tell you?"

"But you said they couldn't play because they're girls, and now you're letting them."

"Well, they're good hitters."

Abe stuck his hands on his hips. "I hit the ball, too."

"So you did," Walter agreed. "All right, you can be on the Blues, too." *He's a better player than Anton anyway,* he thought. "I think Dr. Dan could help coach us, too, along with Mr. Swenson and Per."

"I thought you'd never ask," Dr. Dan said.

Per laughed. "You're going to have the strangest baseball club in town, Walter."

Walter grinned. "Yes, but we're going to have fun!"

Chapter 15
The Showdown

"Girls?"

"On our baseball team?"

"Ha, ha, ha! That's a good joke!"

"Girls can't play baseball!"

"Girls? Yuck!"

Walter swallowed hard and looked around at the Blues. Two days ago at the picnic with the family, it had seemed like a good idea to add Polly and Brita to the club. The club obviously didn't agree.

He glanced across the lot, where Polly, Brita, and Abe were waiting impatiently with Dr. Dan, Mr. Swenson, and Per. Per had said it was important that Walter be the one to talk the club into agreeing to the coaches and the new club members. What if he couldn't convince them it was the best thing? It would be a lot easier if one of the adults told the kids that was the way it was going to be.

He took a deep breath. "We haven't won any matches since the other guys left the club, anyway. What have we got to lose?"

"But, girls!" Eric screwed his face into a scowl.

"Why not let them practice with us tonight," Walter suggested. "Then we can vote on it."

The guys looked at each other. A few of them shrugged, then nodded.

Walter felt like he'd won a war.

The guys had been glad to hear that Per and the men wanted to help with the club. Now he led the group over to where the men and girls were standing and introduced everyone.

"The guys said you can play with us tonight," he told the girls. "Then they'll decide whether you can be on the club."

"That's fair," Brita said.

Polly nodded.

Walter breathed a sigh of relief. Then he saw the way the boys were looking at Mr. Swenson's face. Their eyes were huge.

They look like they've seen a ghost, Walter thought. He glanced at Brita. Her eyes glinted with anger.

She took her father's hand. "This is my papa," she told the boys. "He was in the Washburn A mill explosion."

Walter could see amazement and something like respect for Mr. Swenson replace the fear and horror in the boys' faces.

"I thought everyone in the Washburn A mill at the time of the explosion was killed," Eric said.

"Yes," another boy agreed. "There wasn't anything left of the mill after the explosion. How did you make it out alive?"

"I wasn't in the mill at the time," Mr. Swenson said. "A few minutes before the explosion, another worker and I were having a friendly argument about who should go outside for a bucket of water. I lost the argument, so I was outside when the mill exploded. My friend died. A lot of my friends died."

"My neighbor died in one of the mills that day," Eric said quietly. "I wish he was alive, even if he had scars like yours."

Mr. Swenson put a hand on Eric's shoulder. "I wish he was, too. He was a fortunate man to have a friend like you." He looked around at the boys and smiled his one-sided smile. "Let's practice!"

The men split the players into three groups. One group demonstrated their batting, one their pitching, and one their throwing. At first Per and the men watched until they'd seen each person. Walter could tell they tried to find something good to tell every player. Then they started giving suggestions. The boys listened eagerly and tried to follow their advice.

It was when Polly and Brita showed them how well they could hit that the boys really got interested.

"I wish I could hit that well!" Anton said after Polly had knocked the ball out of the lot.

"I wish you could, too!" Eric told him.

Walter glared at him, then smiled when Anton laughed.

"Dr. Dan and Mr. Swenson taught us how to bat," Polly told them.

Anton grinned. "Maybe there's hope for me yet."

"Tell them what you told us, Dr. Dan," Brita said.

Walter watched all the boys look eagerly at the young doctor.

"Well, the first thing you have to do is learn how something is supposed to be done," Dr. Dan told them.

"We know that. You're supposed to hit the ball with the bat," Eric joked.

"Right. But what does it look like when someone hits the

ball? I mean, when they hit it solid, not just nick it."

Eric shifted his feet and didn't answer. Neither did anyone else.

"Watch when someone hits the ball the way you want to," Dr. Dan said. "Notice the way they hold the bat, the way they swing the bat, and the way their body looks when the bat strikes the ball. Memorize it. Then picture in your mind doing the same thing."

Walter frowned. "That sounds kind of weird."

Dr. Dan smiled. "That's only the beginning."

"What's next?" Walter asked.

"You practice holding and swinging the bat by yourself, without a ball to hit, trying to make your swing and your body move like the perfect hit you have pictured in your mind."

A couple guys swung imaginary bats.

"When you practice, try to remember how it feels to have your body in the right position to hit the ball. After you've done all that, you're ready to practice with a ball."

Eric frowned. "Are you sure this works? Don't you think we should be practicing with a ball all the time?"

Dr. Dan shrugged. "It worked for the girls, but if you don't want to try it, you don't have to."

"Where did you learn this?" Anton asked.

"I've tried it with a lot of things I wanted to learn," Dr. Dan said. "When I learned to be a doctor, for instance. After reading and watching other doctors do operations so I'd know how they were supposed to be done right, I'd practice doing them over and over in my mind, before trying them on people."

Walter shuddered. "I'd rather practice baseball in my mind."

"Me, too!" Anton agreed.

"What did you teach the girls about baseball?" Eric asked Mr. Swenson.

"Well, I told them when they were doing something wrong,

like holding the bat too high. Then I'd tell them how to hold it right."

"That's what you were doing with us tonight," Anton said.

Eric leaned an elbow on Walter's shoulder. "Maybe there's some hope for the Blues after all."

"Even for me," Anton said.

Walter looked around at all the faces as everyone laughed at Anton making fun of himself. The boys hadn't looked this happy in a long time. It wasn't just laughter he saw in their faces. It was something else.

What is it? he wondered.

Then he knew. They believed they had a chance to win again. Maybe not all the matches, but a few. And a few would be enough.

On a sunny afternoon almost three weeks later, Walter, Polly, Anton, and Brita walked through the mill district where the fire had ruined so many buildings. Much of the rubbish was gone, and new buildings were rising in its place.

Some of the businesses that hadn't been completely destroyed were already repaired and open again.

Brita threw her arms up in the air and spun around. "I love Sundays! It's so nice to go to church and spend time with friends instead of staying inside in a dark room and sewing with a lot of other ladies all day long."

Guilt needled Walter. His life was pretty easy compared to Brita and Anton's. "I think it's great you come practice and play matches with the Blues after long days at work, Brita."

Brita smiled. "I like those days best. When my back gets sore from sitting at the sewing machine, I remember I'm going to see all my friends and run and play after work. It makes the days go faster."

"I get to see more of you than I thought I would when you

started working," Polly said. "I'm glad, too!"

"I wouldn't be able to play ball so much if Papa didn't help with the chores around the house," Brita told them. "He doesn't like to do women's work, but he says it helps Mama and me. Besides, doing the chores is good for his hurt arm and hand."

"I wish you didn't have to work in that old sewing factory at all," Polly said.

Brita retied a yellow bow at the end of one of her braids. "Papa says I might be able to quit when he goes back to work."

"Does he know when that will be?" Anton asked.

"No, but the manager at the mill said he will find father a position after the new Washburn A mill opens. He can't go back to his job as an expert miller, though. Not with his injured hand. But he says something good has come from the explosion."

Walter stared at her. "What good could come from something as awful as that?"

"Papa says they've learned how to make flour mills safer," Brita explained, "so maybe other people won't have to die in explosions. An engineer named Barre came and showed the millers a new way to keep most of the mill dust out of the air. Cadwallader Washburn has already put the new units in his Washburn B mill."

"That's great," Walter said.

"My father was offered another job," Anton said. "A good job."

Walter grinned. "That's terrific!"

"He turned it down. It's not at a lumber company or sawmill. He wants to stay in the lumber business. One day, he hopes he can own his own sawmill again."

"I have a feeling he'll make it," Walter said.

Anton nodded. "I think so, too."

"It looks like they're almost done cleaning out the rubbish from the fire," Polly said. "What is Per going to do for a job then?"

Brita's blond eyebrows met over her blue eyes. "I don't know. He's going to try to get back on with the mill when it's rebuilt."

Walter wished he could tell her his secret. His father was hoping to find an opening for Per at the railroad, but he'd made Walter promise not to say anything. He didn't want Per's hopes raised and then not have a job open up.

While the four left the mill district and walked back toward the suspension bridge, Brita told them, "We had the best surprise the other day. Do you remember Lars and his family?"

"Of course," Walter and Polly said at the same time.

Lars's family lived on a homestead in western Minnesota. For years, grasshoppers destroyed their crops every summer. Lars's father had sent Lars and his sister and mother to stay with Brita's family for a while.

"The grasshoppers didn't ruin their crops again, did they?" Polly asked.

"No. They have good crops this year. They sent us barrels of food from their garden and fields! They even sent us some live turkeys and chickens!" Her laugh trilled out. "Wait until you see them, scratching about our backyard."

"They'll be on your kitchen table soon enough," Anton said.

"Yum! I hope so!" Brita answered.

They walked through the tall limestone structures where the suspension bridge met the land and along the walkway out over the Mississippi River.

Walter breathed deeply of the river air. How he loved the smells and sound of the river!

"The last time we were all together on this bridge," Anton said, "was the day of the explosion."

"It feels like years ago," Brita said. "Everything's changed since then."

"Yes," Anton agreed. "Everything."

We've all changed, too, Walter thought. *We're only a few months older, but we've grown up a lot, and we're stronger than we were before. We know now that we can get through really awful things and still have happy times.*

He believed it, but it sounded too corny to put into words to his friends. Besides, he suspected that they already knew it themselves.

Anton leaned against the railing and looked at the water flowing swiftly below. "The Blues have changed, too. We've even won a few matches since Per and the men started helping us."

Polly tipped her chin into the air. "Don't forget about Brita and me."

"Right. You girls have helped, too." Anton looked over at Walter. "You know what I'd really like?"

"What?"

A slow smile played along Anton's lips. "I'd like the Blues to whip Sherman's new ball club."

"So would I!" Polly said.

Brita nodded. "Wouldn't that be fun?"

Walter's own smile grew. "Let's do it."

Chapter 16
On Top of the World

Walter looked across the lot to where Sherman, Jack, and their new team, the Reds, were gathering for the baseball match. He groaned. The Reds were a bunch of strong twelve-year-old boys with confidence shining out of their laughing eyes.

His heart dropped to his stomach. What had ever made him think the Blues, with a bunch of half-good players, a nine-year-old boy, and two girls, could beat a club like the Reds? And losing to the Reds would be worse than losing to any other club.

"Aren't you excited, Walter?" Polly asked, tying on her Blues shield.

Walter tried to make his lips smile. "Sure." Inside he groaned again. *Wait until the Reds find out there are girls on our club.* "I don't even want to think about it," he muttered under his breath, tying on his own shield.

Polly frowned. "What did you say?"

"Uh, nothing. Just talking to myself."

Polly nodded to where Per and the men were talking with Brita, Abe, and some of the other Blues. "Look at Brita hug her father. Isn't that good to see?"

As if she knew they were talking about her, Brita dashed over to them. "Hi! Look, Walter." She pointed to her legs. "Polly and I are wearing blue stockings, just like the boys on the club."

He smiled at her excitement. "They look great."

She grabbed the ends of her braids and wiggled them. "I even wore blue ribbons."

"It looks like you and your father are getting along fine now, Brita," Polly said.

"Yes." Brita dropped her gaze to ground and back up again in a way that made Walter think she was a little embarrassed. "I–I did like you said, Polly."

Polly's brows puckered. "What's that?"

"I made a list of things I like about Papa." She giggled. "At first it wasn't very long, but I thought of new things to add each day. Every time I looked at his face and thought how awful it looked, in my mind I'd repeat one of the things on my list."

"That sounds smart," Walter said.

"Well, I still get mad when other people treat him mean," she admitted, "but now when I look at him, I hardly notice his scars. I just see my papa."

Polly gave her a quick hug.

"Papa likes helping with the Blues," Brita told them. "When I saw how afraid the boys were of him at first, I thought they were going to hurt his feelings. I think they like him, now, though, don't you?"

"They think he's great," Walter assured her. "He's helped everyone on the club learn to play better."

Brita beamed.

"Hey, are we going to play ball here today or not?"

Walter's head jerked up at Sherman's question. He hadn't heard him come up to him. "The Blues are ready whenever the Reds are ready."

Sherman went back to his players.

Polly tossed her brown curls back over her shoulders. "I can't believe I used to think he was nice!"

"Did you notice his shield?" Brita asked. "It's just like the ones we made, only it says 'Reds' instead of 'Blues.' "

Polly's green eyes sparkled. "I guess that's a compliment. But I can't wait to see his face when one of us girls steps up to bat."

I can wait, Walter thought, shaking his head as they giggled together.

The Blues gathered together for a couple last comments from the men and Per. "You have a great team now," Per told them. "You've all improved a lot this summer."

"That's right," Mr. Swenson agreed. "Remember before you bat to see yourself in your mind hitting the ball and watching the ball go where you want it to go, just the way Dr. Dan taught you."

"If you win," Walter's father said with a huge grin, "Dr. Dan and I will treat the entire club to a day at the P. T. Barnum Circus."

The Blues faces broke into wide smiles.

"Hurrah!" Eric yelled.

"Hurrah!" the others chimed in.

Walter grinned at Polly and then at his father. His heart swelled with gratitude at his father's kind offer. Then he glanced across the field at the Reds, and the warm feeling in his chest seeped away. *How can the Blues win against the Reds?*

The Reds were up first. When they saw Polly and Brita take their places in the field, hoots filled the air. Walter wanted to melt right into the dirt. Then he saw Polly's lips tighten together and her jaw jut out. *She and Brita must feel worse than I do,* he thought.

The Reds hit the ball well, like they always did.

The Blues caught the Reds hits better than they usually did and threw better than they usually threw.

When Polly caught a ball that put the Reds out for the first inning, the Reds grumbled. They'd only made one run so far.

Abe was the first batsman for the Blues. Cheers rose from the edge of the lot when Abe picked up the willow bat. The families of Walter, Polly, Brita, and Anton had all come to watch, along with Dr. Dan's family.

Walter straightened his shoulders. *We might not win, but we're going to have fun trying.*

Jack let out a yelp of laughter when Abe stood up to home base. He cupped his hands around his mouth and yelled, "Are the Blues recruiting midgets from P. T. Barnum's Circus now?"

Walter noticed Jack was playing third base for the Reds, the same spot Jack had wanted Walter to take away from Anton. He could see from the set of Abe's jaw that Jack's ribbing made him mad.

"Show him how to play, Abe!" Walter called.

Abe hit the first pitch strong enough to make it to first base.

The next couple batsmen did fine. No home runs were hit, but they didn't strike out and only one was tagged out.

Walter began to feel a little more hopeful. They were playing against the best pitcher in the boys' baseball clubs, and no one had struck out yet!

Polly walked up to home for her turn at bat.

The Reds yelled nasty comments about girl players. Polly's face turned as red as the Reds' socks, but she waited without saying anything while they hooted and jeered. Her courage made Walter fiercely proud.

Sherman walked toward home. Walter met him there beside Polly.

"This has gone far enough," Sherman said with his hands on his hips. "When I saw the girls here before the match, I thought they were only here as kranklets. Girls can't play."

"Why not?" Walter asked.

"Well, it's. . .it's a rule or something."

"No, it's not." Walter hoped his voice sounded calmer and more certain than he felt.

"Well. . ." Sherman waved his arms. "It should be a rule. If it's not written down anywhere, it's because everyone knows it."

"Show it to me in writing, or go back and start pitching."

Sherman turned his back on Walter. "Look, Polly, you're a great little seamstress. You made terrific shields. But you don't want to play baseball. People will think you're a tomboy."

Polly glared at him but didn't say anything.

"What's the matter, Sherman?" Eric called. "Afraid the girls are going to beat your players?"

Now it was Sherman's turn to blush and glare.

"Polly is playing," Walter said. "So is Brita."

Sherman held up his palms. "All right, but don't say I didn't warn you." He walked back to the hurler's spot.

Polly whiffed the first ball.

Walter felt his shoulders tighten. *It's because she's upset by what Sherman said,* he thought. "You can do it, Polly! Remember the picture, like Dr. Dan said!"

She nicked the next ball.

"Come on, Polly!"

The Reds hooted. "Go home and play with your dolls!"

"That's what I'm going to do," Polly called back, "when the match is over and we've won!"

Walter grinned. At least the Blues wouldn't go down without fighting.

The families shouted encouragement to Polly, just like good kranks and kranklets should.

Polly slammed the next ball right past Sherman and second base and into the outfield. Her blue-stockinged legs pumped up and down as she raced toward first base. Safe!

Abe and one of the other Blues players who had been on base when Polly came to bat ran home before the outfielder could get the ball to the Reds catcher.

Walter glanced at Sherman. He was staring at Polly with his mouth open. "Hey, Sherman, what are you standing around for? Let's play ball!" he called.

Eric was next. Sherman tried to strike him out but couldn't.

With Eric on first and Polly on second, Brita came to bat.

The hollers started from the field again. Brita just smiled.

Jack put his hands on his hips and tried to imitate a girl with a prancy walk. The rest of the Reds hooted. Some of the Blues laughed, too.

He does look funny, Walter thought, trying not to laugh.

Brita hit the third pitch squarely. The ball flew between first and second bases, right into the hands of a fielder.

Walter patted Brita's shoulder after she'd tossed down the bat. "Never mind. At least you and Polly showed Sherman and Jack once and for all that girls can whack a baseball. Your father must be proud of you."

She rewarded him with a smile.

Anton was up next. Walter thought he looked tense.

"Hey, Anton!" Jack called. "Vy don't you go back to Sveden?"

Walter bristled at his words and his attempt to imitate the Swedish accent.

Anton whiffed the first pitch.

"Yoost hit the ball!" Jack yelled, teasing Anton with that accent again.

Anton didn't hit the ball. He struck out.

Walter's chest hurt for him. Anton had been playing a lot better lately. He'd hoped Anton could show Sherman and Jack what he'd learned.

At the end of the first inning, Eric said to the other Blues, "When we started this match, I wanted to win. After the things they said to the girls and Anton, I want to win more than ever!"

"Me, too!" another player said angrily.

"Let's play the best baseball we've ever played!" another said.

They all agreed.

The match went pretty well. It was a lot closer than Walter had expected it to be. So close that they were tied going into the last half of the last inning.

"Seven runs to seven runs!" Anton slapped Walter heartily on the back. "This is the best we've played all summer."

Eric grinned. "And it's against the toughest club."

Little Abe brushed a hand through his curly brown hair. "*We're* the toughest club now."

The rest of the Blues laughed.

A little thrill ran through Walter, making him shiver. *Is it true?* He wondered. *Are we the best club now?*

Two outs later, with no one on base and Anton coming up to bat, Walter said in a low voice to Eric, "I guess we're not the best club yet."

Eric nodded, frowning. "There's still the extra innings."

"T'ink yous can hit da ball, Anton? Yah?" Jack called in his poor imitation of a Swedish accent.

Other Reds picked up the taunts.

Anton's jaw set.

Walter's hands clenched into fists.

Sherman made the first pitch.

Anton whiffed.

The Reds laughed and teased him some more.

The Blues families, like true kranks and kranklets, cheered Anton on.

Sherman made the next pitch.

Anton whiffed again.

Walter closed his eyes and tried to ignore the Reds nasty calls.

Sherman made the third pitch to Anton.

Anton hit it!

Foul ball.

Sherman hurled his fourth pitch.

Anton whiffed.

Walter bit back a groan. He heard Eric, beside him, make a loud groan.

The Blues families screamed for Anton. "You can do it, Anton! Hit that ball out of the field!"

With a wide grin, Sherman hurled the ball again.

Crack!

Walter's jaw dropped. He watched the ball soar past the edge of the field and across the street. It dropped into the trees edging another empty lot between two buildings. Then he saw Anton. He was still at home base, staring after the ball! "Run, Anton, run!"

Anton dropped the bat, lowered his head, and ran for all he was worth toward first base.

The Reds players weren't even close to the ball yet. "Keep going, Anton!" Walter cried. He could hear the noisy yells of the Blues and their kranks and kranklets in the background.

Anton reached second base.

Walter could see the Reds were searching for the ball. "Keep running, Anton!"

Anton kept running. His head swiveled toward where he'd knocked the ball, and he missed third base.

"Go back!" Walter waved his arms. "Step on the base!"

Anton ran back, then glanced at the players who'd chased after the ball.

Walter could see a Reds player pull back his arm and throw the ball to another Reds player.

Anton took off for home.

Walter's breath stuck in his chest. His throat ached. Could Anton make it?

The catcher stood over home, waiting for the ball.

Anton dove. Dust flew up around him. His hands slid between the catcher's legs, and Anton grabbed the flour bag that was home. A moment later, the ball smacked into the catcher's hands.

"Safe! You're safe! Way to go, Anton!" Walter raced for home.

So did the rest of the Blues. Anton barely had time to stand up before the club surrounded him, slapping him on the back and throwing their arms around his shoulders.

Sherman, Jack, and the rest of the Reds watched them, their lips turned down at the edges and their shoulders sagging.

"You won it for us, Anton!!" Walter felt like his smile was so big it would split his face in two.

Anton grinned back.

This is the best moment I've had all year, Walter thought. With a start, he realized, *I couldn't be happier if I'd hit that home run myself!*

Anton threw an arm around his shoulders. Walter threw an arm around Anton's shoulders. Together, they started toward the families. The fathers and mothers were smiling and laughing. Walter and Anton looked at each other and grinned.

Days later, Walter and Anton sat with Polly and Brita and the rest of the Blues in one of three circus tents. This was not just any circus. This was P. T. Barnum's Great Traveling Museum, Menagerie, Caravan, and Hippodrome. It was only seven years old, but it was the biggest circus on earth.

The day had started with the huge parade the circus put on. Watching elephants and lions and tigers walking down Minneapolis's streets had sent a thrill through Walter.

Now they'd seen clowns entertain, horseback riders perform stunts, and men and women fly above them on a trapeze, turning death-defying somersaults over their heads.

Walter felt a warm glow in his chest at the nice thing his father had done in taking all the Blues to the circus.

"Thank you," he said to his father, who sat behind them with his mother, Abe, and Judith. Beside them sat Polly's family, Dr. Dan's family, and Brita's family. Walter had to speak loudly to be heard over all the circus music.

His father grinned and said just as loudly, "I think we should all thank Anton. If it weren't for his home run, none of us would be here now. Not even me."

Anton's cheeks grew red, but his smile grew large.

When the show in that tent was over, everyone split up into small groups to visit other parts of the circus. Walter said to Anton, "Let's go see the elephants again. They're my favorite."

Outside the tent, Anton said, "Uh, I know why Sherman and the others left the Blues."

Walter stopped short and stared at him.

Anton kicked at a stone and dug his hands into his trouser pockets. "I know it's because I was such a poor baseballer and Swedish to boot."

Walter swallowed the lump in his throat. "I guess I should have told you. I didn't want you to know."

"Jack wanted me to know. He told me himself."

Walter's hands clenched into fists. "That guy makes me so mad!"

Anton shrugged. "At first, I was embarrassed that he and Sherman and the others disliked me and other Swedes so much that they'd rather leave the Blues than play with us. But. . ." He glanced at Walter and bit his bottom lip.

"But what?"

"You kept me on the club instead of them. I decided if you believed in me that much, I was going to become the best baseballer I could." He hesitated. "Why did you keep me on the club, Walter?"

Walter shrugged. It was embarrassing to put some things into words. "That's what friends do, isn't it? They stick by each other."

The corners of Anton's lips tipped up in a little smile. "Yah. I guess it is."

Walter remembered how hard it had been to choose Anton's friendship over Sherman's. He'd done what he thought Jesus would have done. Walter smiled to himself. It had been hard, and sometimes it had hurt, but in the end it had worked out best.

Together, they ran through the crowds to where people were riding the elephants. Minutes later they were seated on a blanket astride an elephant's wide back. Even through the blanket and his trousers, Walter could feel the elephant's prickly hair sticking into his legs, but he didn't mind. The elephant walked slowly, its trainer leading it. Walter swayed slowly back and forth. The people watching looked small from the elephant's high back.

Walter glanced behind him at Anton and grinned. "We're on top of the world now!"

There's More!

The American Adventure continues with *Lights for Minneapolis.* Judith Fisk and her cousin Abe Stevenson are living in a changing world. Electric lights, phones—these new inventions are making life much easier and a lot more fun. But Abe's father criticizes Abe's fascination with science, and Judith's father doesn't seem to notice her now that there's a new baby in the house. What can Abe and Judith do to make their fathers understand them?